Remember Me

Remember Me

by Irene N. Watts

Tundra Books

Published in Canada by Tundra Books, *McClelland & Stewart Young Readers*, 481 University Avenue, Toronto, Ontario M5G 2E9

Published in the United States by Tundra Books of Northern New York, P.O. Box 1030, Plattsburgh, New York 12901

Library of Congress Catalog Number: 00-131205

Canadian Cataloguing in Publication Data

Watts, Irene N., date
    Remember me

ISBN 0-88776-519-X

I. World War, 1939-1945 – Refugees – Juvenile fiction. 2. Jewish girls – England – Juvenile fiction. I. Title.

PS8595.A873R46 2000   jC813'.54   C00-930415-0
PZ7.W336Re 2000

Irene N. Watts gratefully acknowledges the support of the Canada Council for the Arts in helping her to complete this project.

We acknowledge the support of the Canada Council for the Arts and the Ontario Arts Council for our publishing program.

We acknowledge the financial support of the Government of Canada through the Book Publishing Industry Development Program for our publishing activities.

Design by Ingrid Paulson
Typeset in Goudy by M&S, Toronto
Printed and bound in Canada

1 2 3 4 5 6   05 04 03 02 01 00

For my children and grandchildren

ACKNOWLEDGMENTS

I am grateful to Kathy Lowinger for her encouragement, insight, and in-depth editing; and to Sue Tate, for her meticulous copyediting in "three" languages.

Many thanks to Stephen Walton, Archivist, the Department of Documents, The Imperial War Museum of London, England; to Dorothy Sheridan and Joy Eldridge, Archivists, the Mass Observation Archive, University of Sussex Library, Brighton, England, for their invaluable assistance in my research; to Julia Everett, Geoff Shaw, and to the staff of the White Rock Library, White Rock, British Columbia.

Particular thanks to the following individuals who have shared their stories and remembrances of the time: Hilda Farr, Inge Gard, Margot Howell, Judith Keshet, Joseph and Renate Selo, and A.J. Watts.

Thank you to Noel Gay Music Company Ltd. for permission to quote the lines of the chorus of "The Lambeth

Walk"; to Random House UK Limited for permission to quote the text of the telegram from *Swallows and Amazons* by Arthur Ransome (Jonathan Cape, publisher); and to the Literary Trustees of Walter de la Mare, and the Society of Authors as their representative, for permission to quote from the poem "Five Eyes."

Contents

Prologue

"Open up. Gestapo."

Marianne and her mother collided in the entrance hall. Mrs. Kohn whispered, "Ruth's letter." Marianne disappeared.

"Open up."

The sound of a rifle butt against the door.

"I'm coming."

Marianne heard her mother open the door. The slap of leather on skin. A stifled gasp. Marianne stood in the doorway of her room. She watched the Gestapo officers, their uniforms as black as the night sky, invade their rooms.

Mrs. Kohn put her finger on her lips. Her face was very white. She waited. Marianne stood without moving, watching her mother. Cupboard doors slammed. Drawers crashed. They heard glass shatter.

Something ripped. Gleaming black boots walked toward Marianne. She edged back into her room, picked up her teddy bear, held him tightly.

The officer patted Marianne's head. Turned away.

"Let's go."

They left. Their boots rang out through the building. A car door shut, the roaring engine disturbing the dawn.

Marianne and her mother did not stir until the only sound they could hear was their own breathing. Mrs. Kohn closed the front door, fastened the chain. She and Marianne held each other for a long time.

"My hair – he touched my hair. I feel sick."

"We'll wash it. It's all over now."

"What did they want? Were they looking for Vati?"

"Who knows . . ."

"I hid Ruth's letter."

"Where?"

Marianne kicked off her slipper. The folded letter clung to the sole of her foot.

"You were very brave, Marianne. Now we'll burn it. Come."

Hand in hand, Marianne and her mother walked into the living room. The room looked as if a tornado had hit. Every single book had been dragged off the shelves, and lay on the floor. All her father's beautiful books were scattered, bent, facedown, the pages ripped. His desk was gashed, his chair snapped in two.

Nothing had prepared Marianne for this – not the taunts in the street, nor the smashed Jewish shops, not her mother's anxious warnings not to draw attention to herself, nor her father's disappearance – nothing. And yet, why was she surprised? Why hadn't she expected this? This was what it was like being a Jew in Germany. You couldn't even close your front door against the Gestapo. . . . Marianne watched as her mother packed her suitcase. . . .

"This transport is a rescue operation just for children. A *Kindertransport*. The grown-ups must wait their turn. There are bound to be other opportunities for us to leave."

"You mean, I have to go by myself? No! Absolutely no. I'd have to be crazy to agree to something like that. I won't leave you all."

Mrs. Kohn said, "Marianne, I think you have to. You see, I can't keep you safe anymore. I don't know how. Not here in Berlin, not in Düsseldorf, or anyplace else the Nazis are. . . . One day it may be safe to live here again. For now, we must take this chance for you to escape to a free country."

"Like animals at the zoo"

The guard pushed his way through the corridor. "Next stop – Liverpool Street Station. All change," he called.

The train slowed to a shuddering halt, expelling two hundred apprehensive, weary children. Steam from the engine misted behind them like morning fog. The children climbed down onto the platform. Not knowing what to do next, they formed an untidy line. Eleven-year-old Marianne took Sophie's hand. "Come on, we have to wait with the others. Stay close beside me," she said.

Passersby stared at them curiously. Porters pushing trolleys shouted: "Mind your backs." A few photographers began taking pictures – "Smile," they said. A light flashed, or was it winter sunshine coming through the glass domed roof of the station?

"Like animals at the zoo," Marianne said to the boy standing next to her.

"We'd better smile all the same, make a good impression," he said.

"Wipe your face, Sophie; it's got smuts on it from the train," Marianne told her.

"Are we going to our new families now?" Sophie asked, spitting on her grubby handkerchief and handing it to Marianne, who scrubbed at Sophie's cheeks.

"Soon."

Marianne wasn't ready to think that far ahead. It was only twenty-four hours ago that she'd said good-bye to her mother in Berlin. Today was December 2, 1938, and she was in London – the whole English Channel between her and her parents. The station overwhelmed her with its incomprehensible words and signs.

"A friend of my father's supposed to be meeting me. I don't even know what he looks like. Do you know who's taking you in?" the boy next to her said.

"I don't know anything. I can't even remember how I got here. Don't you feel like we've been traveling for a thousand years?" said Marianne.

"A thousand years, the thousand-year Reich, what's the difference? We're here, away from all that," the boy said. "They can't get us now."

An identification label spiraled down onto the tracks. A woman wearing a red hat climbed onto a luggage trolley facing them. She tucked a strand of hair behind her ear, and spoke to the children in English, slowly, and in a loud voice, adding to the confusion of sounds around them. "I am Miss Baxter. I am here to help you. Welcome to London. Follow me, please."

She climbed down. Nobody moved. Miss Baxter walked slowly along the length of the line, smiling and shaking hands with some of the children. Then she headed up the platform to the front of the line, took a child's hand, and began to walk. She stopped every few moments, turned and beckoned, to make sure the others were following.

"Come on, Sophie, keep up," said Marianne. She could hear some women talking about them and shaking their heads, the way mothers do when you've been out in the rain without a coat.

"See them poor little refugees."

"What a shame."

"Look at that little one. Sweet, isn't she?"

"More German refugees, I suppose. Surely they could go somewhere else?"

Marianne understood the tone, if not the words. Except for "refugee."

"We'll have to try to speak English all the time," Marianne told Sophie.

"But I don't know how. I want to go home," Sophie said.

Marianne was too tired to answer.

A girl dragging her suitcase along the platform said, "This is the worst part, isn't it? Do hurry up, Bernard, we'll be last. Vati said, 'Stay together.'" She called to the small boy trailing behind them, then turned to Marianne and said, "That's my little brother.

Why do boys always dawdle?" They waited for the small boy to catch up.

"Look! A man gave me a penny." Bernard held out a large round copper coin. "He said, 'Here you are, son.'"

"How do you *know* what he said? You don't speak English. You're not supposed to speak to strangers," his sister scolded.

"I suppose they're all strangers here and we are too," said Marianne. "I mean, we don't know anyone, do we?"

"No," said the girl and her lip trembled.

"Sorry," said Marianne. "I only meant . . ." She didn't say any more, and they hurried to catch up to the other children.

The ticket collector must have known they were coming. He smiled and waved them through.

Miss Baxter stopped at last.

"It's clever of her to wear a red hat with that little feather. Like a bird showing us the way," Marianne told Sophie.

"Like Hansel and Gretel," Sophie said, giving a little skip. She'd cheered up again. "Will everyone be nice in England?" she asked.

"Well, it's bound to be better than Germany. Can you imagine the Nazis smiling and holding our hands?" said Marianne.

They followed the red hat into a big room at the end of the station. As soon as they were inside, a woman handed each of them a paper bag with an orange, some chocolate, and a sandwich.

Miss Baxter pointed to rows of slatted wooden chairs lined up on one side of the gloomy room, ready for the new arrivals. The

4

children sat. Across from them, on the other side of the room waiting in a separate section, were the adults. Although it was daylight outside, all the electric lightbulbs were on. The two groups gazed at each other. Some adults stood up, craning their necks to look the newcomers over. A few of them held photographs and were trying to compare the reality in front of them with the posed pictures in their hands.

Miss Baxter announced what was happening in English, and a woman next to her translated her words for the children. "Every sponsor will be paired with a child on my list. We must make sure the names and numbers match. Please wait patiently until you hear your name called."

The woman who spoke German sat at a table in the center of the room and smiled nervously at no one in particular. She was dressed in blue. There was a pile of papers in front of her. Miss Baxter began calling out names, and children and sponsors met for the first time. It went on and on – the names called, the walk under staring eyes, the signing of forms. The endless terrifying anticipation.

Marianne noticed how, sometimes, two children went together. There were nods and smiles and handshakes. Occasionally the adults looked as if they'd expected someone different. The new arrivals followed behind their grown-ups, mostly not turning back to look at the others, who were still waiting to be collected. A few children fidgeted, or whispered. Most sat quiet and watchful.

Marianne held her bag of food so tightly that she could feel the sandwich squish between her fingers. "Do you want my orange?" she asked Sophie. "I can't bear the smell anymore." She knew the bright fruit had been a gesture of kindness – meant to comfort. At this moment, nothing could console Marianne.

Sophie did not answer; she was asleep. She'd pushed her chair very close to Marianne's and was half leaning against her.

The girl sitting on Marianne's other side said, "I'll take your orange if you don't want it."

Marianne gave it to her.

The girl asked, "Is that your little sister?"

"No," Marianne said. "The only thing I know about her is her name and her age. Her mother pushed her onto the train just as we were leaving and asked me to take care of her till we got here. I think it was because I was standing closest to the door. It's worked out alright. She's very good for a seven year old. I won't know anyone when she goes."

"Waiting's horrible, isn't it?" said the girl.

"Sophie Mandel," Miss Baxter called.

"That's you, Sophie. Come on, you've got to wake up." Marianne pulled Sophie to her feet.

A pleasant-looking woman in a gray coat and hat said to her in German: "*Nicht stören* – don't wake her. I can carry her."

Sophie woke up anyway.

"Hello, Sophie. I am Aunt Margaret, a friend of your mother's. I've come to take you to your new home."

Sophie put her arms around Marianne's neck and hugged her, as if she didn't want to leave her behind.

"Good-bye, Sophie. She looks very nice," Marianne whispered, and kissed her cheek.

Sophie went off bravely, carrying her doll and her rucksack. Marianne saw the lady smile at the little girl and heard her answer a question. Sophie turned at the exit and waved to Marianne. It was all Marianne could do, not to cry. She blew her nose, pretending she'd caught a cold.

Why do I mind Sophie leaving? It's not as if we're even related. Everyone's being separated. The boy she'd talked to in the line had been one of the first to go, and Bernard's sister had left too, with an elderly man and woman. She'd tried to explain to Miss Baxter about staying with her brother, but the couple were anxious to leave and didn't let her finish talking. Marianne saw the girl turn round to look at Bernard. He hung his head and refused to look up. He sat slumped like that for ages, even when the lady in blue came over to him and put a note in his hand. "Your sister's address," she told him.

Miss Baxter called his name. A cheerful young woman collected him. She had a small boy with her who looked about Bernard's age. The boys began making faces at each other almost immediately. He'd be alright.

The girl she'd given her orange to had left with a woman in a fur jacket. The room was almost empty. *Suppose no one comes for me? Is there a special room for unclaimed children?* Marianne wished she'd never let her mother talk her into coming here. She planned her first letter home:

Dear Mutti,
    I'm still in Liverpool Street Station. Please write to me here.

Perhaps Miss Baxter would give her a stamp.

Marianne tried to push this moment out of her thoughts. She closed her eyes, hoping the sick feeling in her stomach would go away.

· 2 ·

"I'm sorry I took someone's place"

"Are you Leah Stein?"

Marianne opened her eyes and saw Miss Baxter stooping beside her.

"I must have fallen asleep. Sorry." She spoke in German, then remembered where she was. "My name is Marianne Kohn."

Miss Baxter checked the number on Marianne's identification label, and scrutinized the remaining names on her list. Marianne saw that most of them had already been crossed off.

"I'm afraid there isn't a Marianne Kohn listed. Nothing to worry about," she said reassuringly. "I'm sure we can sort it out. Miss Martin speaks German and you can explain to her. Follow me."

Marianne carried her suitcase to the table where the lady in blue was sitting. Speaking in German, the woman asked, "Is there a reason why there isn't a record of your name here, my dear?"

"I came with the group from the Berlin orphanage. It was all sort of last minute because two of the girls got measles." It was a relief to speak in German. But before Marianne could continue, the ladies began to confer.

"The orphans are supposed to stay together in the hostel at Dovercourt in Harwich, till homes can be found for them. I don't know how this child got separated from the group. We'll have to make arrangements to send her back to them."

"Send back? *Zurück schicken?*" Those were the only words Marianne understood. "Please, no. *Ich bin Jüdisch* – I am Jewish. No send back." *Don't these ladies understand? But how can they? They don't know about the Gestapo; they haven't been on the train out of Germany.* Marianne sat on her suitcase, and hid her face on her arm.

Miss Baxter said, "No one is going to send you back to Germany."

Miss Martin continued, "You misunderstood. Now, tell us slowly, calmly, all about the measles and why you are not with the other orphans. Please don't worry; I promise you are quite safe."

Marianne looked up at their kind faces and said, "My mother helped out at the orphanage. Two of the girls got measles and couldn't travel, so the supervisor said I could come instead. I'm sorry I took someone's place."

"Now I understand, but I'm sure they'll come when they're better. Don't worry about that," said Miss Martin.

Miss Baxter wrote Marianne's name on the list and showed it to her. "There, you're quite official now."

A tall thin woman wearing a coat with an elegant fur collar approached. In a voice that matched her sharp features she announced, "I am Mrs. Abercrombie Jones. Is this girl Leah Stein?"

Miss Martin turned to Marianne and said quietly in German, "Just wait, dear."

Marianne sat very still, watching, trying to understand what was happening.

"I know you've been waiting some time, Mrs. Abercrombie Jones. I'm afraid Leah has not arrived. She may have changed her mind, or been detained in Holland. This is Marianne Kohn."

The lady ignored the introduction and looked round the room as if Leah might be hiding somewhere. Marianne noticed that she was the last girl. All the rows were empty except for four boys sitting together in the back.

"Marianne does not have a sponsor," Miss Baxter said. "It seems quite providential in a way. You did specify a girl, didn't you?"

The woman's mouth set in a straight line. "This is all rather haphazard, isn't it? The girl's aunt wrote me that Leah is a responsible domesticated fourteen year old – the school leaving age. My husband and I agreed to take in a refugee to help around the house. Why wasn't I notified?"

Miss Baxter said, "I'm sure you're aware, Mrs. Abercrombie Jones, that this is the first *Kindertransport* that has been allowed to leave Germany. We must be grateful that so many refugee children at risk have arrived safely." Somewhere a station clock struck 3:00 P.M. It echoed in the cavernous room. "It's getting late. I'm sure Marianne will fit in splendidly. Won't you, Marianne?"

11

"Please," said Marianne, totally confused, but sensing this woman did not seem to want her. *She reminds me of that horrible Miss Friedrich at school.*

"How old are you?" the lady asked.

Marianne stood up and curtsied. "I am eleven and one-half years old." She'd practiced this sentence. She could also talk about the weather, and she knew how to say "good morning," "good-bye," "how do you do," "please," and "thank you." She knew lots of words. She'd been taking lessons for two years – the English Miss had been a good teacher, and English had been one of her favorite subjects at school before the Nazis had expelled Jewish students. *Was it really such a short time ago?*

Marianne took her father's German/English dictionary out of her bag. She'd found it lying facedown under his desk the night after the Gestapo had left their apartment. The leather binding was scratched, but the pages were fine after she'd smoothed them out. Her father's name was written inside the cover – "David Kohn." The publisher's name was Hugo. Vati used to say, "Bring my little Hugo and we'll look it up," when he helped her with her English homework. It was a small pocket dictionary, which fitted into her palm, and feeling it was as though she were holding Vati's hand.

I won't cry; please God, don't let me cry now.

Miss Baxter said firmly, "I'm sure Marianne will suit you beautifully, Mrs. Abercrombie Jones." She patted Marianne's arm.

The lady asked Marianne, "Do you speak English?"

Marianne nodded. "Yes, please. I speak a little."

Mrs. Abercrombie Jones smoothed the fingers of the leather gloves she was wearing. "She looks young for her age. Our house is not suitable for children; however, as I've told everyone we are sponsoring a refugee girl, I shall keep my word."

"Thank you so much. Good-bye, Mrs. Abercrombie Jones."

Miss Baxter turned to the last boys waiting to be called.

"Come along, Mary Anne," said the lady, not even attempting to pronounce Marianne's name correctly.

Marianne followed Mrs. Abercrombie Jones. *She doesn't look very motherly. I hope we get to like each other.*

· 3 ·

"Welcome to London"

Outside Liverpool Street Station, the city of London soared out of the fog. "Here I am in the biggest, most wonderful city in the whole world." Marianne wrote a letter in her head to her mother. "A big red double-decker bus just passed by, and guess what, Mutti? It says BUCKINGHAM PALACE on the front. Imagine, I could just climb onboard and go right to the palace and see the king and queen and the two little princesses – Elizabeth and Margaret Rose."

Marianne remembered how she and her cousin Ruth used to read every bit of news they could about the royal family. The winter coat Marianne was wearing today was in the same double-breasted style that she and Ruth had so admired when they saw the princesses wearing it in the photograph in the *Berliner Illustrierte*. Her mother had cut down an old coat of her father's to make the coat fit her, and had finished it just before

Kristallnacht – the Night of Broken Glass. It felt strange wearing Vati's coat and having no idea where he was hiding.

"Watch where you're going, ducks." A uniformed sleeve steadied her. Marianne looked up into the smiling face of a helmeted London policeman.

"I'm so sorry, officer. She's just arrived from Germany." Mrs. Abercrombie Jones sounded as if she were apologizing for a badly behaved puppy.

"No harm done. Good day, Ma'am. Welcome to London, Miss."

"Taxi," called Mrs. Abercrombie Jones. A shiny black automobile halted at the curb.

My first taxi ride, Mutti.

"Twelve Circus Road, St. John's Wood, please." Mrs. Abercrombie Jones settled herself in the center of the leather cushions and pointed for Marianne to sit on the pull-down seat under the driver's window.

Marianne sat down. *Circus? Does the lady live in a circus? She doesn't look like anyone who has anything to do with animals. Perhaps I could help hand out tickets. She definitely said "circus."* Opa loved attending the circus – long ago, when Jews were still allowed to go. One day he'd told her all about the elephants, how they held flags in their trunks and waved them in time to the band. Then Opa had laughed and whispered, "I hear they're training the seals to bark '*Heil Hitler*.'" He'd put his finger to his lips in warning. "Walls have ears."

Marianne looked at Mrs. Abercrombie Jones, and was sure she wouldn't make jokes. The lady noticed Marianne staring. Their eyes met. Marianne smoothed her coat over her knees, and pulled up her kneesocks. She had to make a good impression. *I'll be good and polite. It'll be easy to behave perfectly. My English isn't good enough to answer back yet.* She smiled at Mrs. Abercrombie Jones.

Mrs. Abercrombie Jones cleared her throat. Marianne looked up apprehensively. *Suppose I can't understand what she says to me?*

"I'm dying for my tea, aren't you?"

"Yes," said Marianne, hoping this was the correct reply.

"Where did you learn to speak English, Mary Anne?"

"I learn in school."

"In school? Oh yes, of course, school." She paused, frowning a little. "You will have to go to school, I suppose. Monday, if possible." She sighed.

"I like so much go to school," said Marianne.

"Good," said Mrs. Abercrombie Jones. She took a small gold compact out of her handbag, and powdered her nose.

Marianne could smell her perfume, like lilies of the valley. Mrs. Abercrombie Jones undid the fur collar of her brown coat, and Marianne saw that she wore a strand of pearls and a pale blue cardigan over her cream-colored silk blouse. Her skirt was of brown tweed.

She'd write Mutti everything, tell her about the smart clothes, and the fine shops, and the statues and parks. But the harder Marianne looked at the passing scene through the taxi window, the more blurred the city appeared. Mutti's anxious face kept coming between Marianne and the view. Her mother looked the way Marianne remembered her in those last precious few minutes in their apartment in Berlin. Marianne could still hear her voice, "Everything will be different, Marianne – the language, the customs, the food. You're bound to be homesick at first. You must try to fit in, to adapt. Be grateful, darling. How kind people are to give a home to a child they don't know. It may take a while for us to get a visa to come to England. Who knows? You might be the one to find someone to sponsor us; you're certain to meet lots of English people. All we need is an offer of work, and an address. We must have an address you see, darling, to get a permit. Why don't you try and see what you can do?"

She'd said it with a little smile, and patted Marianne's cheek, so that Marianne needn't take the request too seriously. But Marianne knew she'd been very serious.

Marianne had said, "Of course I will, Mutti." Now she repeated the promise silently.

The taxi stopped. "'Ere you are, Ma'am, 12 Circus Road."

Marianne was startled; her thoughts had been so far away.

Mrs. Abercrombie Jones paid the driver, counted her change, and gave him a coin. He touched his cap, smiled at Marianne, and drove off.

Marianne looked around for signs of animals. It was just a street. Not a circus at all. She couldn't even see a dog.

Mrs. Abercrombie Jones pushed open a black wrought-iron gate, and Marianne followed her along a short path of paving stones to the door. There was a neat hedge around the square front garden and two flower beds.

Marianne had never lived in a house before, except on holiday when she'd stayed with her grandparents in their house. In Berlin, the people she knew lived in apartments.

It was very cold. A maid in a black dress and white apron and cap answered the door. She said, "Good afternoon, Madam," and helped the lady off with her coat.

"This is Mary Anne." Mrs. Abercrombie Jones pronounced it like two words, the English way. "And this is Gladys. Gladys has been with us since she was fourteen – isn't that right, Gladys?"

"Yes, Madam. Welcome," Gladys said. She had a freckled face and a snub nose. Her smile was real, not just polite.

"Tea in ten minutes, Gladys. Come along, Mary Anne. I'll show you to your room and you can wash and unpack before tea."

Marianne couldn't work out if all these words needed a yes or no, please or thank you. So she said nothing at all, and followed Mrs. Abercrombie Jones.

"This is the drawing room; it looks over the front garden. It gets the sun in summer." Mrs. Abercrombie Jones spoke loudly to Marianne, as though she were deaf. Marianne understood one or two words, and guessed the rest.

Mrs. Abercrombie Jones opened the first door in the wood paneled hallway, and Marianne just had time to notice a dark pink couch with matching armchairs, several occasional chairs, and a pink and green rug centered on the polished wood floor.

"This is the dining room. The kitchen is at the end of the corridor. Tomorrow you will eat your meals there with Gladys."

She went up the stairs, her feet silent on the brown wool carpet. Marianne followed. When they reached the landing, Mrs. Abercrombie Jones showed her the bathroom.

"Do you have running water at home?"

This seemed a strange question. Marianne thought it was safe to say yes.

The lady seemed surprised at her response. They passed closed doors. Then more stairs – this time uncarpeted. Marianne's suitcase felt as heavy as if it were full of bricks. The linoleum squeaked under their feet.

Mrs. Abercrombie Jones switched on the light. "Gladys sleeps next door. Come down when you're ready." She ran her fingertips lightly along the window ledge, checking for dust, and went out.

Marianne said "sank you" to her retreating back. Mrs. Abercrombie Jones did not reply.

· 4 ·

"Where this house, please?"

Everything was green – light green. Marianne felt as if she were underwater. The bed stuck out from a green painted wall. The heavy cotton counterpane was green and white. A wooden chair stood at the bottom of the bed. Marianne put her suitcase on it, carefully, so as not to dirty the towel that hung over the back of the chair.

Under the window was a small wooden chest of drawers, also painted green, and there was a narrow wardrobe for hanging her clothes. There was no bookshelf, but that was alright. There'd only been room to pack one book – her parents' early Hanukkah gift to her – and, of course, her precious dictionary.

There was no bedside table or lamp. A green fringed lamp shade covered the electric lightbulb, which hung from the center of the ceiling. A picture on the wall was of a smiling lady in a white dress, sitting under a tree and reading to a small blonde girl.

• *"Where this house, please?"* •

Marianne drew the thin curtains. It was dark outside, but the light from the kitchen window below gave a glimpse of the shadowy garden. She could just make out one small tree, bare of leaves, and a shed. Marianne shivered and drew the curtains again, to hide the night.

"This is the loneliest place in the world." Marianne spoke out loud to break the silence. *If I run away, who'd come to look for me? Who'd care enough to find me?* Marianne breathed deeply, forcing herself to be sensible. *Mutti will come soon and get me. I can bear it till then.*

Marianne unpacked quickly. She placed the picture of her parents, which she'd put in her shoulder bag at the last minute, in the center of the chest of drawers.

It didn't take long to put her socks, underwear, and sweaters away and hook her dressing gown on the back of the door. She hung her two skirts, two blouses, and best velvet dress in the wardrobe. There was a mirror inside the door. She looked just the same as she had in Berlin. Somehow she'd expected to look more English. Finally, she picked up her worn teddy bear and held him against her cheek for a moment, before stuffing him under the sheets with her pajamas.

Marianne gave her hair a quick brush, and checked herself again in the mirror. Was it her imagination, or did her face reflect the green of the walls? Marianne closed her bedroom door softly and went to wash her hands and face in the bathroom. Anything to delay the moment of going downstairs.

Voices came from the dining room. The door was ajar. *Am I supposed to knock or just go in?* Marianne stood in the doorway and waited to be noticed.

A dining table and four chairs with carved backs stood in the center of the room. There was also a sideboard, with a radio on one end and a cut-glass decanter and matching tumblers on the other. Two more chairs stood against the wall, which was patterned with wallpaper of green leaves and little bunches of grapes.

Green must be the family's favorite color.

The other wall, the one facing the window, was dominated by a tall cupboard with glass doors. The shelves were full of china. Marianne tried not to think of the mess there'd be if the Gestapo came in the night and smashed it. Her fingertips tingled as she remembered the feel of the sharp edges of broken plates. She heard again her mother's urgent whisper: "Careful, you'll hurt yourself." Deliberately, Marianne willed herself to return to the present.

I wonder why we don't have tea at the table. I hope I don't make crumbs. The fire looks so nice and warm I'd like to curl up in front of it and go to sleep.

Mrs. Abercrombie Jones looked up and saw her. "Come in and say 'how do you do,' Mary Anne."

A man dressed in black, with a stiff round white collar, stood by the mantelpiece, his back to the fire. He was talking to another man, who was smaller and thinner, wearing a business suit. They both stopped talking and looked at Marianne.

Mrs. Abercrombie Jones sat in an upholstered chair in front of a coal fire. Beside her was a tea trolley on which were delicate china teacups, with a rose pattern to match the large teapot. There was a plate of thin bread and butter, and another of finger sandwiches. A dish of raisin scones and a layered jam sponge were arranged on a tiered silver cake stand.

Nodding towards the small thin man, Mrs. Abercrombie Jones said, "This is my husband, Mr. Abercrombie Jones, and this is Reverend James, who has dropped in for tea especially to meet you, Mary Anne."

Marianne curtsied and said, "How do you do." Just the way she and Vati had rehearsed.

The man in black said to Marianne in German, "I like to walk in your beautiful country. I love the Black Forest." And then he turned to Mrs. Abercrombie Jones and said something Marianne didn't understand.

Marianne had never been to that part of the country. It was full of Nazis; she'd heard ugly stories. *Who is this man . . . is he a party member?* He spoke with a heavy accent.

"*Wie war die Reise?* How was the journey?" he asked.

Why is he asking about the journey? Have the Gestapo recruited him as a spy?

She thanked him cautiously, "*Gut danke.*"

Again the man turned to Mrs. Abercrombie Jones and spoke in English.

Marianne wondered if she should make a run for it, try and find Miss Baxter, but how?

Mrs. Abercrombie Jones smiled at the man and said, "Oh, well done, Vicar. Now do sit down everyone please, and let's have tea."

Marianne sat on a small narrow chair and took a sip of the pale brown liquid that Mrs. Abercrombie Jones handed her. This was not the kind of tea they had at home. She was used to drinking it black, with a slice of lemon. She'd never tried it mixed with milk and sugar.

The man who might be a spy spoke to her in German again. In spite of his English accent, she could understand him quite well. *If he asks me about my parents, I won't say one word. Hitler has spies everywhere. Why did Mrs. Abercrombie Jones take me? She was expecting someone else.*

The man said, "Mrs. Abercrombie Jones does a lot of charitable work in our little community. Does your mother work, my dear?"

She'd been right – the interrogation was continuing. Marianne determined to give nothing away.

"Mrs. Abercrombie Jones is the first one in our congregation to offer sanctuary to a refugee. You are a lucky girl."

What is this word "congregation"? He'd said it in English. *Is it some kind of political party? He looks very kind, but that doesn't mean much. It would be like the Gestapo to send a kind-looking spy to fool me.*

Mr. Abercrombie Jones said, "May we *please* speak English?" He offered the bread and butter to Marianne.

The grown-ups talked to each other between mouthfuls of cake and sandwiches. Marianne managed to swallow one small triangle of bread, and then was offered cake by the "spy." She didn't dare refuse. It was very good cake, but Marianne couldn't swallow. This was worse even than the day she'd lost her front door key. She didn't know whether she wanted to cry, or be sick. Her stomach hurt, the way it always did when she was upset. It hurt a lot. *I want Mutti.*

Gladys came in with a plate of jam tarts. A piece of coal fell from the fire onto the brown tiled hearth. Everyone turned to look, and while Gladys dealt with it, Marianne slid the cake off her plate onto her lap and covered it with her handkerchief.

At last tea was over. The adults made good-bye noises and went into the hall.

"Good-bye, Mary Anne. *Auf Wiedersehen.*"

"Good-bye," said Marianne and stood up.

The moment they left the room, she threw the cake into the fire and watched it flare up for a moment. The voices in the hall continued loud and bright. Gladys came in to clear the tea things.

"Mary Anne," said Mrs. Abercrombie Jones loudly, "go into the kitchen with Gladys and help her with the dishes, then come in and say goodnight."

Gladys gestured at Marianne to follow.

In the kitchen, Gladys put a tea towel in her hand. She made signs and gestures as she spoke. "I'll wash, you dry. Put the things on the table. I'll put them away." She pointed to the table and repeated "table."

Marianne already knew that word. She liked the simple way Gladys communicated. Gladys had strong, very red hands. She worked quickly. "All done. Off you go – say goodnight to Mrs. Abercrombie Jones. Go on, then."

Marianne would have much preferred to go straight up to her room, but it was only polite to say goodnight, and she had an important question to ask.

Marianne knocked on the dining room door.

"Come in." Mr. Abercrombie Jones put down his paper.

"I must write my mother. Where this house, please?"

Mrs. Abercrombie Jones stared at her. Her husband looked over the top of his paper, said "London, England," and laughed as if he'd said something funny. "Here, I'll write down the address for you," he said.

Even English handwriting looked different.

"Also, please, your name?"

The lady said, "Mr. and Mrs. Abercrombie Jones."

He wrote some more. "Bit of a mouthful, isn't it? Tell you what? You call me Uncle Geoffrey; and my wife, Aunt Vera. Go on, try it. I'll write it down for you."

His wife said something to him, and did not look pleased.

Marianne said, "Onkel Geoffrey," sounding a soft *J* as in the German *Ja*. Then, "Aunt Wera."

The newspaper went up over the Onkel's face, and Marianne could see the paper shaking. *He's laughing at me. What's so funny?* Vati always said she had a good English accent.

Aunt Vera said, "Mary Anne, in English we say V; it is a hard sound, and Uncle Geoffrey's name is pronounced with a G. Do you understand?"

Marianne nodded. She was so tired. "Please, Aunt Wera, I need stamp," and she held out one of the big round pennies that had been given to her for the ten marks each child had managed to exchange in Harwich.

Uncle Geoffrey waved the penny away, took out his wallet, and gave her a stamp.

"A present."

"Sank you. Goodnight."

"Goodnight, Mary Anne," Aunt Vera said with a sigh.

The Onkel grunted something behind his paper.

Marianne closed the door and went upstairs. Back in her room, she undressed quickly and tried to get under the bed-clothes. The blanket and sheet were tucked in so tightly under the mattress that she could hardly pull them free. *How do people get into bed in this country?* The sheets were so cold they felt damp. She longed for her cosy feather bed.

Marianne got up again, put on her dressing gown and socks, and took her writing paper from her suitcase. Then she sat up on the bed and began her first letter home, carefully copying out her new address.

She wrote: "Dear Mutti and Vati," and stopped. Even writing a letter presented problems. *Should I write to both my parents? What about my grandparents?* If the Nazis got hold of her letter, they'd find Mutti and shout: "Where is your husband?" She knew Opa would shout back: "Leave us alone," and they'd all be dragged off to prison.

Marianne crossed out "Vati." Now that Mutti was moving to Düsseldorf to live with Oma and Opa, they could share her letter and get in touch with her father when it was safe to do so. *If only*

I'd had a chance to say good-bye to them all. Marianne wondered how her father felt when he found out she'd left for England. *How could our lives have changed so fast? One minute we were all together and the next, I'm here, in this cold green room, in a house where people talk loudly at me and laugh at things I can't understand.* The linoleum creaked outside her door. *Is someone coming in to say goodnight, to tuck me in?* No one did. Doors shut. The house was silent.

I'll write my letter tomorrow. Marianne got into bed, pulled the covers over her head, and held her poor skinny teddy bear tightly. She talked to him the way she used to when she was a little girl. "We're on holiday abroad, that's all. The reason you feel strange is because it's only the second night away from home. You'll soon get used to it."

If she kept her eyes closed and concentrated on teddy's familiar old fur smell, home didn't seem so far away.

Marianne half whispered, half sang the words of the lullaby her mother used to sing to her:

> Sleep my baby sleep,
> Your Daddy guards the sheep.
> Mother shakes the gentle tree
> The petals fall with dreams for thee
> Sleep my baby sleep.

Teddy's thinning fur was wet with tears before the song was over.
They slept.

· 5 ·

"I'm fine"

Marianne woke up on her first Saturday in England and stared at the overhead lightbulb. It was on. She must have fallen asleep before she'd switched it off.

She was starving. When she went down to the kitchen, it was lovely and warm. A place had been set for Marianne at one end of the scrubbed table.

"Porridge," said Gladys, as she placed a bowl of some kind of gray pudding in front of Marianne. "Here, I'll show you." She sprinkled sugar over the top and poured milk from a glass bottle, then swiftly cut triangles of toast and arranged them in a silver toast rack on a tray and left the room.

Marianne eagerly spooned up the porridge. It was lucky that Gladys wasn't there just then because the first mouthful almost made Marianne gag. Quickly she scraped the food into the sink and turned on the tap, so that by the time Gladys came back, Marianne was sitting down again, the empty bowl in front of her. She could almost smell the warm crusty rolls her mother always served for breakfast, with homemade black cherry jam. She wanted to be with her so much that she had to dig her nails into her palms to stop from crying.

Marianne tried to imagine what her mother was doing. She might be in Düsseldorf by now. After they'd got the notice from Mrs. Schwartz saying she wouldn't allow Jewish tenants in the building anymore, Mutti had said she'd leave as soon as she'd packed up.

"I don't think I can bear it," Marianne said, and only Gladys' stare of surprise and her "what did you say?" made her realize she'd spoken aloud, and in German. *I mustn't do that again. Do the other kids from the transport feel this mixed up?*

Mrs. Abercrombie Jones walked into the kitchen, her coat over her arm.

"Good morning, Mary Anne."

"Good morning, Aunt. . . ." Marianne had forgotten how to pronounce the "aunt's" name.

"Aunt Vera," prompted her sponsor. "Gladys, we are leaving now."

Leaving? Who is leaving? Leaving means going away. Am I being returned to Liverpool Street Station?

Marianne heard her name – she was supposed to do something. *What is it?* Marianne knew she had to pay more attention. She'd missed most of their conversation. She didn't know why her thoughts kept drifting.

Mrs. Abercrombie Jones left the kitchen.

Gladys put a duster in Marianne's hand. "You dust downstairs. Come on, I'll show you."

Marianne was afraid she might break something, or put things back in the wrong place, and only dusted around objects, not daring to move anything. At last she was done and could go upstairs, make her bed, and settle down to write home.

Marianne didn't want to upset her mother. She was determined to hide her homesickness and how much she wished she'd never come. Instead, she tried to write cheerfully.

12 Circus Road,
St. John's Wood,
London, NW8
England

3 December, 1938

Dear Mutti,

I arrived safely. I liked the boat. I have my own room at the top of the house. There is a garden. I have plenty to eat and can understand a lot of English words. Mrs. Abercrombie Jones, the lady who took me in, says I can start school on Monday.

I was so happy when I found your letter. I'll remember what you wrote about looking at the same sky even though we are living in different countries.

The scene in the train compartment, when the Gestapo emptied the contents of the suitcases on the floor, flashed in front of Marianne. She'd never forget the greedy eyes of the man who'd stolen Werner's stamp album. Funny how she could remember the names of every one of the children she'd traveled with, yet found it so hard to recall Aunt Vera's.

Marianne tried not to think about the way the Gestapo officer had hit her bear across his knee, the way he'd wrenched off the head of Sophie's doll. She relived the moment when she'd edged her foot forward to cover the letter from her mother that had slipped out of its hiding place in the sleeve of Marianne's party dress.

Marianne got out of bed and ran across the cold floor to get her mother's letter from its hiding place in the lining in her suitcase. She smoothed the page carefully and read her mother's words:

My dearest daughter,

You will be far away from me when you read this letter. It is so hard to let you go. I watched you sleeping last night as though you were still a small baby. I wished I could change my mind and keep you here, but that would be too selfish.

You are going to a better, safer life. Here, there might be no life at all. One day you will understand why I had to let you go. If only we had more time together. Someone else will lengthen your clothes, buy you new shoes, tie your hair. Did it grow into curls as you always hoped it would? I miss you already. I will miss having to nag you for coming in late.

I will miss complaining about your messy room, or you not doing your homework. I will miss your first grown-up party. Will you still love to dance?

Please try to understand, Marianne, why I must miss all your growing up, all these special things. Because, I love you. I want to give you the very best life there is, and that means a chance to grow up in a free country. Here there is only fear.

I pray that you, and all the children whose parents send them away, will find loving families. I will think of you every day, and wish for your happiness, and that you will grow up into a good honorable person.

Wherever you are, wherever I am, at night we will be looking at the same sky.

Always, your loving Mutti

She folded up the letter carefully and put it back in her suitcase. She knew she would never own anything more precious than this. Marianne had to wipe her eyes before she could continue writing her own letter.

"I'm fine." *Will Mutti know this is a lie? I'm not fine. I'm afraid.* Not afraid of being beaten up in the streets by gangs of Hitler Youth, nor the kind of fear she'd felt when she saw the body of the man tumbling down from the window of his house in the square. This was a kind of fear she'd never experienced before – wanting to cry all the time because she didn't know what to do, or what was expected of her; not knowing how long it would be before Mutti could come for her; afraid because she did not belong anywhere and was trying not to show how strange she felt in this English house.

"Please give my love to <u>everyone</u>." Marianne underlined the word twice. "Don't worry about me. I know you'll try to come here soon.

Much love and many kisses,
From Marianne"

When Marianne asked Gladys where to post her letter, Gladys said, "Turn right at the end of the street. The pillar-box is around the corner; it's red." Marianne found the way easily.

She'd be brave, walk on and explore a bit. There was nothing else for her to do. She hadn't seen any books or games when she was dusting.

Marianne walked along the High Street. The shops were crowded, and so were the pavements. Some windows already had Christmas decorations in them. Marianne looked for a bookshop, and found one. It was much bigger than the one her father used to work in. She looked eagerly at the display. At the top of a pyramid of books was a familiar red cover – *Mein Kampf* by Adolf Hitler. The black swastika looked huge. It stared at her.

Suddenly Marianne began to run, pushing through the shoppers as if Hitler himself were after her. She did not stop until she had a pain in her side, and her lungs hurt. She leaned against some park railings to catch her breath. She must stop being so silly. Her father always talked about "freedom to choose." This was a free country, so bookshops could sell anything they wanted to. But why choose that book?

Marianne went inside the park. It didn't look like a place to be afraid of. A river wound in curves through the green lawns. Fat ducks swam among reeds, or sheltered under overhanging trees. Unexpected fountains, small ornate bridges, and paving stones in intricate patterns surprised her. A small girl bowling a red hoop just avoided crashing into her. "Be careful," called the girl's mother. Marianne knew what the words meant from the woman's gesture. She thought longingly of the times she'd groaned when Mutti told her to be careful. She'd give anything to hear it now.

An old lady was feeding pigeons. She made room on the bench for Marianne to sit down, then carefully poured some bird seed from a paper bag into Marianne's hand. A pigeon alighted on Marianne's wrist. A small boy with a red kite ran around making bird noises and the pigeons scattered. The old lady said, "Goodbye, dear," and left.

It was getting cold; other people were leaving. This was the first time Marianne could remember sitting on a bench that wasn't marked FOR ARYANS ONLY – the first time she'd been in a park where Jews could sit anywhere they liked, not only on yellow benches. It was late; the afternoon was over.

When she found her way out of the gates, she didn't know which way to go. She must have come out through a different entrance. It was almost dark. *I'm lost.* An English policeman walked past her. *Is it safe to speak to him?*

"Please," Marianne sobbed.

He turned and walked back and looked at her. "Now then," he said, "no need to cry. Did someone hurt you?"

Marianne hadn't realized she was crying. She shook her head, wiped her eyes, and fumbled for the piece of paper with her address on it. The policeman took it. He spoke too fast for Marianne to understand more than a few "lefts" and "rights."

"Please, I don't understand," she said.

"Follow me," said the policeman, and walked her all the way home to her gate.

Aunt Vera's horrified face, when Gladys opened the front door and said, "Here she is, Madam," told Marianne that she must have seen the policeman. "Where have you been? What will the neighbors think?" She sounded very angry. Not worried – angry – embarrassed angry.

"Sorry," said Marianne. "I lose the way."

Aunt Vera talked loudly at her for a long time before sending her into the kitchen for tea. Marianne was in disgrace.

· 6 ·

"Old enough to know better"

Aunt Vera came into the kitchen, where Marianne faced an unfamiliar Sunday breakfast of fried bread, bacon, and eggs. "Good morning. Finish your breakfast quickly, Mary Anne. Church begins at 10:00 A.M. Gladys, dinner at the usual time, so you can finish early. Mary Anne may eat with us in the dining room today." Mrs. Abercrombie Jones left the kitchen and shut the door.

Marianne carried her plate to the sink. "I wash dishes?" she asked.

"No, thanks. Better get ready for church," said Gladys.

"Please, what is 'church'?"

Gladys turned to her with a look of shock.

Now what have I done? This was the trouble in a new country — you never knew when you said or did the wrong thing.

Aunt Vera called out impatiently, "Mary Anne, put your hat on. We'll be late."

Marianne walked behind Aunt Vera and Uncle Geoffrey along the High Street to a beautiful old gray stone building, with a tall spire. Organ music greeted them. Marianne knew immediately why Gladys had looked so horrified when she'd asked what "church" was. "Church" meant *Kirche*. She'd forgotten the word, that's all. She used to pass *Neuekirche* – New Church – on the way to visit her father's bookshop, and the French Church was near *Unter den Linden* on the *Französichstrasse*. This was the first time she'd been inside one.

They sat down in one of the long shiny pews. Men and women together. Black leather prayer books were on a ledge in front of them, and a cloth-covered footstool was on the floor at each person's place. Marianne was so busy looking at the stained glass window of Jesus wearing long white robes, surrounded by sheep, that she was late standing up. Aunt Vera gave her a small push. Everyone sang, even Aunt Vera and Uncle Geoffrey. Then they all sat down again.

A man who looked strangely familiar, dressed in black robes covered by a sort of white overshirt, began to speak. He went on for a long time and Marianne dozed. She opened her eyes when he stopped, and there was a great shuffle while everyone knelt on the little footstools.

Suddenly Marianne remembered where she'd seen the speaker before. It was the "spy in black," the one who'd come to greet her on Friday for tea.

Marianne tugged at Aunt Vera's sleeve. "Please, Aunt Wera . . ."

"Not now, Mary Anne," Aunt Vera hissed. "The vicar is speaking."

Marianne tried to stifle nervous laughter, but couldn't quite manage it. How could she have thought this man was a spy!

Aunt Vera gripped Marianne's arm and said, "*Sh*." She bent her pink face over her book.

Marianne imagined what she'd write to her mother about her first visit to church. It was beautiful and seemed like a nice quiet place to be, even if it wasn't a synagogue. She was sure God wouldn't mind her being here!

On the way out her "spy" shook hands with everyone. "I am glad to welcome you to our church, my dear," he said to Marianne in his accented German.

Marianne nearly giggled again. She bit her lip and looked down.

On the way home Aunt Vera said, "You disgraced me, Mary Anne. Everyone was looking at us. You are old enough to know better. Well? Say something."

Marianne was lost in the jumble of words.

Uncle Geoffrey looked at Marianne. "Tell Aunt Vera you're sorry," he said sternly. "Say sorry." He raised his voice.

"I'm wery sorry, Aunt Wera."

"Ver, Vera – speak properly, Mary Anne. You're not trying! Thank goodness you start school tomorrow."

They walked back in silence.

Gladys had set Marianne a place in the dining room, but reset Marianne's place in the kitchen after Aunt Vera spoke to her.

· 7 ·

School

That Sunday night Marianne was too excited and nervous to sleep. She'd been in England only three days, and tomorrow was the first day of school.

She got out of bed and checked her clothes again. The linoleum felt as cold to her bare feet as if she were outdoors. Marianne set herself a test to ensure a smooth day at school. She opened the window, ignoring the sharp December wind that blew in. Slowly, she counted backwards from one hundred. She had to do it without shivering, or start again. She did it the first time. *Everything will be alright now.* She closed the window gratefully.

When Marianne finally went to sleep, she dreamed of her math teacher in Berlin. He was dressed all in black; his high boots shone. There was menace in each threatening step that marched towards her. His mouth was twisted in hatred, and opened and closed angrily, but she could not hear his words. His hand reached out for her teddy bear, and raised it to show the class before hurling the bear through the window with a force that shattered the glass pane.

"No!"

Marianne woke up. *Did I scream?* The house was still. "Only a bad dream." She could hear her mother's voice in her head, imagine her forehead being stroked.

Next morning Marianne walked beside Aunt Vera, who had been giving her instructions ever since they left the house. She couldn't get the nightmare out of her mind.

"Mary Anne, are you listening? Answer me, please."

"Pardon, Aunt Wera?" Marianne said.

"I said, oh, never mind. Here we are. I'll come to the office with you."

They crossed the playground, which was full of laughing, skipping girls. Some boys kicked a football; one almost ran into Mrs. Abercrombie Jones. She gave him her iciest look.

Aunt Vera handed Marianne over to the secretary along with a note, said good-bye, and left.

Marianne spelt out her name, and managed to remember her new address.

"Did you bring your records?" the secretary asked.

Marianne looked at her. *Records?* Thank goodness she'd brought her dictionary. She looked up the word. Marianne shook her head.

The secretary said, "Please ask your mother to send them."

A door opened and an imposing-looking lady, with white hair, entered briskly. She read Aunt Vera's note. "You must be Mary Anne Kohn." She shook hands firmly with Marianne. "I am Miss Barton, the headmistress. I am going to take you to your new class. Come along," she said matter-of-factly.

The morning was strange, not a bit like school in Berlin. The teacher gave her a desk in the second row and a curly-haired girl called Bridget was assigned to stay with her for the day and show her what to do.

Assembly was in the big hall. The teachers sat on the stage, and the headmistress stood in front, at a lectern. "Good morning, school," she said.

All the students stood and answered, "Good morning, Miss Barton."

Then they sang a song about Jerusalem being built in a green land. Marianne thought of her father raising his glass and saying, "Next year in Jerusalem." Perhaps they'd all be together in London soon.

Miss Barton said, "We are delighted to welcome a new student to Prince Albert Elementary School. Mary Anne is a refugee from Germany, and we hope she will be happy here."

Every head swiveled to look at her.

Bridget nudged her and whispered, "Don't worry."

Marianne concentrated on pretending to be somewhere else, but felt her cheeks going red all the same.

The morning passed easily. It was good to get back to a

routine. Marianne was so busy she didn't have time to miss her mother. Did that make her a bad person? Shouldn't she feel miserable all the time?

Bridget said, "Must be awful to start school so late in the term – poor you." She shared her milk with Marianne at milk time because she hadn't brought any money.

Even math was alright, nothing like the nightmare. The teacher wrote problems on the board that seemed to involve a greengrocer, a customer, and many questions about carrots, potatoes, and onions, and how much they all cost if one added more, or took some away. The teacher saw Marianne desperately looking up words in her dictionary, and called her up to his desk. A boy in the back row snickered and whispered something about Huns. He was given extra homework. Mr. Neame sent Bridget down to the "infants" to get a box of English play money, and he wrote on a card what all the money represented, and told Marianne to learn it:

ONE FARTHING = 1/4d OF ONE PENNY.
ONE HALFPENNY = 1/2d OF ONE PENNY.
TWELVE PENNIES = ONE SHILLING.
TWENTY SHILLINGS = ONE POUND.

(Tomorrow, she would buy two bottles of milk – one for Bridget. Milk was 1/2d a bottle.) There was also a threepenny piece and a sixpence, two of those making one shilling. There was a big silver coin and that was called half a crown, eight of those making a pound. It was very complicated. Marianne wondered if she'd ever understand it all.

In the afternoon there was drawing, and music. The first thing Marianne noticed when she entered the music room was the writing on the blackboard – it was in English and German:

O Christmas tree, O Christmas tree, With faithful leaves unchanging;
O Tannenbaum, O Tannenbaum, Wie treu sind deine Blätter!
Not only green in summer's heat, But also winter's snow and sleet,
Du grünst nicht nur zur Sommerzeit, Nein, auch im Winter wenn es schneit,
O Christmas tree, O Christmas tree, With faithful leaves unchanging.
O Tannenbaum, O Tannenbaum, Wie treu sind deine Blätter!

The teacher said, "Today we are going to learn the words of 'O Christmas Tree' in the original German. Mary Anne can help us with the pronunciation. Would you read the German text please, Mary Anne."

Everyone waited. Marianne wasn't quite sure what she had to do, so she didn't do anything. The teacher picked up the wooden pointer from her desk and raised it. Marianne bit her thumbnail. *Is the pointer for me?* She hid her hand; her cuticle was bleeding a bit. The pointer rested on "*O Tannenbaum.*"

"Begin please, Mary Anne," said the teacher and smiled at her.

By the time she'd read to the end of the first line, Marianne was transported back to a Berlin winter. She remembered standing on tiptoe in the street as a very little girl so that she could look through the windows at the Christmas trees, with their white candles of flame making halos around each green branch. Her mother had made her hurry away long before she'd gazed her fill at the brightness. "It's not polite to stare into someone's home," she'd said.

Great soft flakes of snow clinging to coats, resting on the cobbles, on the streetlights. Flags hung from every building. Flags, red as blood, their centers snow-white circles and, in the middle, swastikas black as ebony. Red and white and black, like the story of "Snow White" by the Brothers Grimm.

Marianne's heart pounded so loudly she was sure everyone else could hear it. Her voice shook. She just managed to finish reading the last line.

"Thank you, Mary Anne. Now all together, class," the teacher said, and raised her pointer again.

At the end of the day they were given homework – some spelling – a whole list of words connected with winter: Arctic, blizzard, chilling, freeze, glacial, icicle, numb, shepherd, snowdrift, snowstorm. They were told to write a sentence to show the meaning of each word.

That night Marianne looked up the words in her dictionary and wrote: "Aunt Vera's face is glacial when she looks at me. I feel numb with sorrow without my mother."

It took her hours to finish the homework, and her head ached.

"My mother . . . is most wonderful cook"

"Tomorrow when you come home from school," Aunt Vera said one afternoon in late January, "you may help me serve tea to my friends. Change your blouse and brush your hair before you come in."

"Yes, Aunt Vera. Many ladies are coming?" asked Marianne.

"Mrs. Brewster, Mrs. Stephens, and Mrs. Courtland – my bridge group."

Tomorrow. Marianne hurried upstairs. She had lots to prepare: write down her mother's address in Düsseldorf, check out words in her dictionary, and practice her pronunciation. One of those ladies might have work for her parents!

Next day, after scrubbing the ink off her fingers with pumice stone, she handed round plates of thin bread and butter, scones, and sandwiches. Gladys had given her an encouraging wink before she entered the dining room.

Marianne waited for her opportunity to speak.

"Your frock is darling, Phoebe," Mrs. Stephens said.

"Oh, do you like it? I'm so glad. I've found the most wonderful dressmaker. A little Jewess who's set up shop in the Cromwell Road. She works out of two rooms, my dear, only arrived last year from Vienna. Had her own salon there, I believe. Lost everything to the Nazis. She uses a borrowed sewing machine. Her prices are quite reasonable and she'll copy any design." Mrs. Courtland paused and sipped her tea.

"Please," said Marianne, "my mother can sew also, and she is most wonderful cook, and my father is very clever and speaks good English. They want to work in England." Marianne held out the paper on which she'd printed her mother's address. "Here is the place for you to write."

Aunt Vera took it, crumpled the paper into a ball, and dropped it onto the tea trolley.

Then everyone began to speak at once, as if Marianne had done something awful, like spilling the tea.

"Are your parents in Vienna too, my dear?" asked Mrs. Brewster.

"Rather sweet and brave of her to ask. Don't be cross, Vera," said Mrs. Stephens.

"Of course, Dora's been with us for years. I don't think she'd approve if I brought a *foreigner* into her kitchen. No one bakes like your Gladys, Vera, my dear. You are so fortunate. Do let me try one of those little scones now," said Mrs. Courtland.

Aunt Vera found her voice at last. The lines of her mouth looked pinched. Marianne sensed her anger. "We can manage now, Mary Anne. Please ask Gladys to bring in more hot water."

After the guests had left, and Marianne had finished helping Gladys with the drying up, Gladys said, "Don't know what you did, but you're to go and see Mrs. Abercrombie Jones."

Marianne hesitated outside the dining room. She rubbed the sore place on her thumb, where she'd bitten the skin. Then she walked in and stood in front of Aunt Vera.

"I am very displeased with you, Mary Anne. I understand that you miss your mother, but I cannot allow you to make a nuisance of yourself. You embarrassed me, *and* my friends. What you did is like begging."

"It is wrong to try save my parents?" Marianne asked softly.

"Don't exaggerate, Mary Anne. They must wait their turn like other refugees. It is not a question of saving, but of good manners. Now, I am waiting for an apology, and a promise not to behave like this again in my house."

"Sorry," said Marianne.

"And, I've been meaning to speak to you about your hands."

"They are quite clean, Aunt Vera. I brush them."

"You must stop biting your nails, and the cuticles. It is an ugly habit. Try harder in everything, Mary Anne. Now go and finish your homework. Goodnight."

Instead of doing her homework, Marianne began a long delayed letter to her cousin Ruth. She'd emigrated to Amsterdam with her parents last November. Uncle Frank was a furrier and had a job to go to in Holland. That's why they'd got a visa and been allowed to leave Germany.

12 Circus Road,
St. John's Wood,
London, NW8
England

25 January, 1939

Dear Ruth,

I memorized your address, didn't want to risk any-one finding it on the train. Now that I'm in England fears like that seem far-fetched, but we know they aren't, don't we?

I bet you thought I'd forgotten you – of course I haven't. But you can imagine the panic when we had less than twenty-four hours notice that I was coming to England. Settling down here and learning different rules and being *nagged* in two languages from both sides of the Channel isn't my idea of paradise. Mutti writes constantly that I must be grateful and obedient. In England they expect you to be quiet and invisible, but for different reasons than in Berlin. Not to be safe, but to be polite.

I've been here seven weeks now and I've learnt more English than I did in two years in Germany.

The first couple of weeks I thought I'd die of homesick-ness, and it's still hard sometimes, specially when I'm bursting with news and no one's there to listen.

School is mostly alright. Some of the kids tease me and imitate my accent, but it's normal teasing, you know, not the throwing stones kind. I haven't found any other Jewish students. If they're there, they are keeping very quiet about it. I can't very well stand up in Assembly and say, "Excuse me, is there anyone here who's Jewish?" I don't expect there were enough Jewish homes to go around for all the *Kindertransport* children. It was a bit of a muddle, especially as no one was expecting me. Did I tell you, I was on the very first one ever?

Bridget, a new friend, helps me with English. Her father is a doctor who left Ireland at eighteen. In Ireland the different religions are always quarreling and the English and the Irish – at least some of them – don't like each other. Bridget's been called names, even though she was born here. We have a lot in common. I'll miss her when she goes to another school – a grammar school for girls. They have beautiful school uniforms, and always have to wear a black velour hat with the school badge when they go out. The motto is in Latin and means 'Trust in God.' I do trust Him, but I wish He'd hurry up and bring my parents over. Aunt Vera (Mrs. Abercrombie Jones, who took me in) is not a great substitute for a mother, even if I was looking for one, which I'm not!

Write soon and tell me all your news. Love to you all from your loving cousin,

Marianne

Marianne had just sealed the envelope, when she heard the doorbell. Footsteps came running up the stairs. A moment later,

Bridget knocked at her door. "Ready for your English lesson? I brought Pa's *Times* – you can practice reading from it."

"Bridget, I have a great idea," said Marianne.

"What?" asked Bridget.

"Promise no word to Aunt Wera," Marianne said.

Bridget groaned. "Vera, V like vampire, W is like in water. Yes, I promise."

"I have to find work for my mother. I will knock on doors and ask. Aunt Vera must not find out. Will you help me write what to say?" Marianne asked her friend.

"It's a brilliant idea – of course I will," said Bridget.

"Sank you," said Marianne.

"*Th*, put your tongue between your teeth like this, thank you," said Bridget.

"Thank you," said Marianne. "Is better?"

"Much," said Bridget. "We can put the advertisements under doors, even if no one's home."

"Hurry, Bridget, I can't wait longer," said Marianne.

"Let's look what they say in the *Times* under DOMESTIC SITUATIONS REQUIRED. You read it, Mary Anne. It's good practice for you."

Marianne said, "This one's from a girl in Berlin! From *Turinerstrasse*. Listen: 'I am a girl of eighteen who likes dressmaking and is fond of children.' We can write like this for my mother?" She almost shouted.

"Easy. Just change the words a bit. I'll write it down for now, and type it up on Pa's typewriter later. I'm a bit slow, but I'm accurate. We'll go together. Two's much better than one, and if there are watch dogs, I have a great affinity with animals," Bridget declared.

Marianne and Bridget jumped up and down in excitement.

Gladys came hurrying up the stairs. "Mrs. Abercrombie Jones wants to know if you are deliberately trying to give her a headache?"

"I'm very sorry, Gladys, please tell Aunt Wera."

Gladys closed the door behind her.

"Listen," said Bridget. "Gifted Jewish dressmaker . . ." she started to write.

"Say good cook, no, wery good cook," said Marianne. "Love the children."

Bridget interpreted this as: "Gifted Jewish dressmaker, excellent cook, fond of children, wishes to come to England as a domestic."

"Now, what about your father – what can he do in the house?" asked Bridget.

"Nothing. Vati cannot boil water for coffee. He only likes to read." Marianne smiled, thinking of her father.

"No problem," said Bridget. "We'll say 'Husband works as a gardener / handyman.' That means he cleans shoes, and cuts grass, rakes leaves, that kind of thing. . . . Now give me the address, and I'll say 'Please write immediately to. . . .'"

Marianne printed her mother's name and address. "Thank you, Bridget."

"I'll start right away. How many do we need?" Bridget asked.

"More than one hundred?" Marianne asked hopefully.

"Tell you what – I'll begin with twenty-five, and we'll see how many replies we get."

They ran downstairs.

"Good-bye, Mrs. Abercrombie Jones. I've finished Mary Anne's English lesson. I have to go now," said Bridget.

"Thank you, Bridget. Please give my regards to your parents."

"I will," said Bridget. "And Mother sends her regards to you, too."

"You would never know that child comes from Irish stock. She has beautiful manners. You may go and help Gladys bring in the tea things."

"Yes, Aunt Wera . . . Vera."

Marianne heard Mrs. Abercrombie Jones say, "Do you think she does it on purpose, Geoffrey?"

· 9 ·

Miriam

On Saturday after lunch, Marianne and Bridget set off to deliver the first batch of DOMESTIC SITUATIONS REQUIRED.

"We'll start at the top of Avenue Road – those big houses looking over the park. We'd better go to the back, where it says TRADESMEN'S ENTRANCE," Bridget said.

"You think we look like tradesmen?" Marianne giggled to cover up her nerves.

"Mary Anne, we're not doing anything wrong. It's not like we're asking for money."

Bridget had this knack of knowing what Marianne was really thinking. "I'll do the first one," she said.

"No, I must do it. Look, this house is number five, my lucky number," said Marianne. "Even when I was small, I used to make bargains with myself. I would make a kind of promise. Walk to the corner, keep head up. If men in uniform come, if I keep walking, if I'm brave, something good will happen."

"I do that all the time too. Alright, you ring this bell; I'll do the next one."

There was no reply, though they heard the wireless playing though the kitchen window. Marianne pushed the note under the door. The next two houses were closed up, the milk crates sitting empty on the back step.

Then they got three answers one after the other. In one house a very grand butler wearing a striped green waistcoat said, "I will make sure this gets delivered, young ladies."

"Let's do one more," said Bridget, and then walk over to Gloucester Place. "We don't want to put all our eggs in one basket."

"Sometimes," Marianne said, "English drives me mad. Where is the basket with the eggs?"

Bridget's face went red and she laughed so hard the tears streamed down her face. "It means we'll have a better chance of success if we don't concentrate on only one street," Bridget said, when she could speak again! "It's a figure of speech – understand?"

Marianne groaned. "Thank you," she said, exaggerating the *th* sound.

She took the last note for Avenue Road, rang the bell, waited a moment, then pushed her paper under the door. It opened suddenly and she almost fell over the threshold.

"Little girls, vot you doink here?"

Marianne straightened up to face a plump young woman with dark hair tucked under a maid's cap. She wore a pinafore over her striped uniform. Their advertisement was in her hand.

"Come inside, it is cold. My name is Miriam Levy. I vork here."

Bridget hesitated, but Marianne pulled her arm. "It's alright. Trust me." To the woman in uniform, she said, "I'm Marianne Kohn from Charlottenburg, Berlin. I'm trying to bring my parents to England. Do you speak German?" Then she put out her hand and the woman shook it, nodding her head. Marianne saw that she was only a few years older than they were.

Miriam replied in German, "I'm so glad to meet you. I came to England at the end of last October. I'm trying to bring my mother over too. My father was arrested after I left. My brother is in Sachsenhausen Concentration Camp. He is only seventeen." She pressed her hand against her lips to stop their trembling.

"My father was there for a while. I don't know where he is now," Marianne said.

Bridget coughed several times to remind them of her presence.

"Oh, Bridget, I'm so sorry. It was rude of us not to speak English, but Miriam's a refugee too. Miriam, this is my best friend, Bridget O'Malley. She's helping me."

"I am wery pleased to meet you. Come sit. I just now was making the coffee. Madam is shopping. I pour you a cup, or you like better tea?"

"Tea, thank you, Miriam," Bridget replied.

"Coffee, please," Marianne said gratefully. The smell instantly brought back memories of home: poppy seed rolls on the blue and white plate; Mutti and she drinking coffee (hers mostly milk); Mutti's look of mixed horror and amusement as Marianne confessed to walking down *Kurfürstendamm*, watching the elegant ladies perched outside on little gold painted chairs at the pavement *Konditorei* tables; imitating the waiter's voice as he offered them whipped cream on huge portions of apple cake – "*Mit Schlag Gnädige, Frau?*"; the chestnut trees in blossom in spring, rows and rows of them; the lights that never went out in the city; the words of the language she was born with that she didn't have to struggle with every minute. Marianne looked at Miriam. *Does she feel this kind of homesickness, too? For what we've lost, for what we've never had because we aren't Aryans?*

Miriam offered them biscuits from a tin.

"You go ahead, speak German. I don't mind," said Bridget.

Miriam said, "No, I never vant, but perhaps some words – if I don't know how to say."

Marianne asked her, "How did you manage to come over?"

Unconsciously, Miriam replied in her native tongue, "I met Mrs. Smedley in Berlin in 1936. She was on holiday with her husband, for the Olympic Games. I was eighteen. She asked me for directions to her hotel. I walked with her, then she invited me in. I explained it was not allowed because I was Jewish. She took my arm and said, 'I am an English tourist; no one will stop me.' So brave! We had coffee in her suite. She told me if I ever wanted to go to England, if things got worse, to write to her. When my father's business was taken away, and I lost my job as his bookkeeper, my mother told me I should write to Mrs. Smedley. It was an opportunity. I did, and she sponsored me. She is very kind. I make mistakes, but she makes allowances for me. My friend Hannah lives in London too, but she lives in one little room. When she wants a bath, she must pay sixpence for the hot water." Miriam poured more coffee. "She works in a household where they are mean to her. I think she is often hungry."

"Why don't the Jews in England do more to help?" Marianne burst out in German. "Sorry, Bridget, just this one question."

Miriam said, "They help all they can, but there are so many of us trying to get out of Europe. Mrs. Smedley says in England less than one percent of the population is Jewish. A few are rich, but most are like us – poor, or immigrants, trying to bring their relatives to England. I'll keep this paper, Marianne. I might hear of a place for your mother."

The front doorbell rang.

"That will be Mrs. Smedley. I must go." This time she spoke English.

"Good-bye. Thank you," the girls said, and went out the back way.

On the way home, Bridget said, "You looked funny in there."

"That's not very polite." Marianne was offended.

"I didn't mean funny 'funny,' only different. I haven't heard your name said like that before. Marianne, it sounds nice. Look at the time – Pa has fits if I'm home after dark."

"Thanks for coming with me, Bridget."

"Think nothing of it," said Bridget grandly.

They went all the way back without stepping on the cracks of the pavement even once. It couldn't hurt, and it might help bring Marianne's parents over to England more quickly.

"So far away"

Two weeks later, Marianne heard from Ruth.

> 107 Leidsegracht, Apt. 5,
> Amsterdam,
> Holland

> 6 February, 1939

Dear Marianne,

It was wonderful to hear from you at last. I'm quite jealous. It must be so much more romantic emigrating across water, instead of to a country where you can just walk across the border. Not that anyone can do that anymore.

When we found out that your train had actually stopped for a couple of hours in Holland, Mother got in a state, and cried. She went on and on about her little niece and no one to meet you, and if she'd known, she could have brought you food parcels. Why is it that mothers think we're going to die of starvation the moment we leave home? Incidentally, the rumor is that English cooking is terrible. I hope that's not true – you're quite skinny enough.

Seriously, Marianne, I think you are very brave to go so far away by yourself, away from us all. Papa says the farther the better. He doesn't think we can ever be far enough away from Hitler. But parents are difficult. When I talk about my plans, I'm told I don't know anything. Poor you being told off by everyone.

I joined a Youth *Aliyah*. The idea is to train us to go to Palestine one day. We *should* have a country of our own, then no one could hurt us anymore. I know it would be a hard life, living communally on a kibbutz and sharing everything, and working on the land, but it's worthwhile, don't you think? At our meetings we learn songs and dances and have a lot of fun. In September we are going on a three-day camping expedition. Mother says I'll "grow out of it," that I'm too spoilt for such a hard life. Papa wants me to be apprenticed to a furrier. He says, "Coats you always need." Not my idea of a fulfilling life. I'm determined to get to Palestine somehow.

I like the sound of your new friend. Perhaps we'll all meet one day. Meanwhile, Mother says you are all in our prayers. We talk about you often.

Keep in touch, please.
Your loving cousin,
Ruth

One week later Marianne received a postcard from Czechoslovakia. The pictures were of the gleaming spires, medieval roofs and turrets of Prague – Vati had always told her it was one of the most beautiful capitals in Europe. She didn't know anyone there. The card was printed, and undated. It said:

Hello Marianne,

This traveler has found a beautiful city, and hopes to stay awhile. There are cafés, galleries, and bookshops. Some still sell our favorite books. I often think of that fine supper I shared with you and your dear mother.

Love and greetings to you both,
D.

D for David. It's from Vati. He's safe! Why has he disguised his identity? Isn't Prague free? She was glad, though, that he was being so cautious. There were spies everywhere. Now, he'd surely come to England. How clever of him to give the Nazis the slip.

Marianne wished she could ask him how he crossed the frontier. It was like a miracle. She twirled around the room in stocking feet. Linoleum was wonderful for sliding. And she had to keep warm somehow. No heat reached the bedroom at all.

Marianne huddled back down on her bed and read Vati's card again. She thought of the last time she'd seen him. She could smell the onions frying, see her mother's flushed cheeks, feel her own cheek pressed against the rough texture of Vati's jacket as he hugged her good-bye after supper.

The last time she'd seen him was when he was on the run from the Gestapo. The pit of her stomach felt as empty as it had then, that awful moment after he left again to go into the cold night to hide goodness-knows-where. *Oh, Vati, I hope you're warm and happy now. I hope you know how much I love you.*

"Mary Anne, where are you? Gladys needs help with the silver," Aunt Vera called.

Marianne went down into the kitchen and attacked each piece of cutlery as if she could make all the bad people in the world disappear by polishing them away.

Gladys said, "If all refugees work like you, there won't be any jobs left for us." She smiled, but Marianne was hurt. It seemed if you were a refugee, whatever you did was wrong.

That evening Aunt Vera said, "I see someone sent you a card from Prague. Do you have friends there?"

"My father."

"Oh, I see. Is he on holiday?"

"Beautiful place," said Uncle Geoffrey. "Medieval city, cobbled streets, and all that. That glass decanter set was made in Czechoslovakia."

Marianne looked at them. *Holiday? Don't they realize what is happening?*

"Mary Anne, are you listening? Answer the question."

"Sorry," said Marianne. "No, not holiday. He's running from Hitler, like me."

"Well, that's hardly the same thing. Have you finished your homework?"

"I have ten more words to learn for the spell test."

"Spelling. Run along then, goodnight."

Three weeks later the newspaper headlines declared: NAZI TROOPS MARCH INTO PRAGUE.

Uncle Geoffrey said, "They just let them walk in. What do you expect? Foreigners – no backbone." He made the word "foreigners" sound like a disease.

Marianne borrowed books about Czechoslovakia from the library. There was one with a street map of Prague. She wanted to imagine the places where her father might hide. There were castles and cottages in the countryside. Someone might help him. *First Austria, now Czechoslovakia – where will the Nazis go next?*

That night Marianne woke up and found herself at the top of the stairs. She didn't know how she got there. The next night

Gladys found her wandering again, and helped her back to bed.
Afterward, she didn't remember anything about it. Gladys told
Mrs. Abercrombie Jones next morning.

"What's all this nonsense I hear about you walking about the
house in the middle of the night, Mary Anne? Are you ill?"

"No, Aunt Vera, I'm quite fine," said Marianne, realizing that
for once Aunt Vera was not angry.

"Too much tea, Gladys. From now on, Mary Anne is to drink
nothing at all after six o'clock."

That night Marianne put books in front of her bed, so that
she'd fall and wake herself up. But it didn't work. She told Bridget
about walking in her sleep.

"We'll just have to try harder to get a visa for your mother.
Look, I've typed up ten more copies of our advertisement," she
said.

Marianne replied, "Thanks, Bridget, but you see it's no good
looking for a job for a couple anymore. The Nazis have taken
over in Czechoslovakia; it'd be hard to escape."

"If he can get out of Berlin, he can do anything," Bridget said
comfortingly, but the next day she changed the words on the
advertisement, so that there was no longer any mention of
"gardener / handyman."

"Where did you get those shoes?"

Every evening after tea, Marianne spread a double sheet of newspaper on the scullery floor and cleaned the household's shoes. Sometimes yesterday's paper was so interesting that she'd still be there an hour later. Last week there was a story about a famous film star, and Aunt Vera had come in and stopped her reading "such rubbish."

"No wonder you walk in your sleep. I forbid you to read the paper from now on. Finish the shoes and go to bed."

Shoes were a constant problem for Marianne. She wore her Wellingtons most of the time. In school she changed into brown plimsolls, like the other girls.

The Wellingtons were made of black rubber and came to her knees. The boots reminded her of the Gestapo. All the children wore them. In spite of wearing two pairs of socks, her feet were still always freezing.

Marianne rubbed her feet together to stop them itching. She had developed big red bumps on her heels and toes. Chilblains, Gladys called them. They were a fact of life in England, like porridge for breakfast. When her feet warmed up, they got hot and itchy and swollen. Her fingers were red and cracked, too. Gladys told her to leave the dishes for a few days to give her hands a chance to heal.

If Marianne complained to Aunt Vera, she knew she'd be told not to fuss, so she said nothing. She discovered that if she slid under her icy sheets at night and went to sleep before she got warm, her feet didn't keep her awake.

The shoes she'd brought from Berlin were getting awfully tight. They hurt her toes and she couldn't straighten them.

Last Sunday on the way to church, Uncle Geoffrey, who hardly ever noticed her or made personal remarks, said, "Mary Anne, you're hobbling about like an old lady. Put your head up, shoulders back." Before she had a chance to explain that her shoes pinched, the vicar was greeting them. Aunt Vera didn't refer to the incident and Marianne didn't like to ask for new shoes.

Tomorrow there was a jumble sale. Marianne decided she'd donate her outgrown shoes. The sale was for a really good cause — for the Spanish villagers who'd been bombed by the Fascists.

Next day she put her shoes in the box marked JUMBLE. On Friday, school finished an hour early, so they could all go to the gym. Marianne had sixpence to spend. Perhaps she'd be lucky and find a pair of shoes to fit her.

The gymnasium was crammed full – students, teachers, parents, and relatives. One table was doing a huge trade serving tea poured from a big metal urn, at a penny a cup. Marianne made her way to the used-clothes stall. Next to it was a table with secondhand books. She'd just take a quick look. Bridget's birthday was next month. Arthur Ransome's *Swallows and Amazons* was lying at the back of the table, half covered by a Latin dictionary. Marianne picked it up. It was in really nice condition, and only cost twopence. She leafed through it quickly, and came to the part where the children got a telegram from their father: BETTER DROWNED THAN DUFFERS, IF NOT DUFFERS WON'T DROWN.

The first time she'd read that, she couldn't find a translation for "duffers." Now she knew it meant 'someone useless.' It was the kind of thing her father might have said to her in his joking way. Wasn't she like Roger and Kitty and the others? All alone, and she was making decisions as best she could. She *had* to buy the book for Bridget's birthday. They'd both read the library copy, and Bridget had said, "I'd love to have my own." Bridget had become such a good friend, always doing things for her. This could be something Marianne could do to please her. Sometimes Marianne worried that when Bridget went to grammar school, she'd find another best friend, that things wouldn't stay the same between them.

"Are you going to read the whole book before you buy it?" Her math teacher was smiling at her.

"Sorry, Sir," said Marianne and gave him a threepenny bit.

"How much change would you like, Mary Anne?"

"One penny, please," she replied.

Teachers could never resist a chance to teach, even after school.

Mr. Neame said, "Well done," and handed her the book and the change. That left fourpence. It didn't seem much to buy a pair of shoes. Even the worn-out ballet slippers were sevenpence.

"What are you looking for?" the woman helper at the shoe stall asked her.

"Walking shoes, size, um . . . three (that was the size of her Wellingtons) . . . or three and a half. Thank you," Marianne said.

"There's a big box of shoes under the table; I haven't had time to price them yet. Have a look and see if you can find what you want."

Marianne rummaged through them, finding nothing in her size.

"How about this pair? They should do you, nice leather, and only a bit scuffed. They'd soon brush up. They're hardly worn. Let you have them for ninepence."

"Thank you, but I've only got fourpence left."

"Sorry, dear. I don't think I can let them go for that. Tell you what, if I haven't sold them by the time we close at 7:00 P.M., I'll let them go for a bit less. Come back then."

Marianne did some quick calculations: she had fivepence at home, but she needed stamps and toothpaste. She stood there undecided.

Mr. Neame called her over. "Mary Anne, is there a mathematical difficulty I can help you with?"

Suddenly Marianne felt the whole gymnasium go quiet as if, at that moment, everyone was listening. *How can I explain that I have no shoes, that there's no one to tell what any mother would know?* She could feel herself blushing.

"It's . . . that I did not bring enough money to spend, Mr. Neame. It doesn't matter, thank you. I must go now." Marianne started to edge away.

Mr. Neame said, "Do you know what a short-term loan is, Mary Anne?"

She shook her head.

"Suppose you want to buy a shop, but don't have quite enough money to pay for it. You could borrow the money from a bank, and sign a paper to promise to pay the debt by a certain date. Now, how much do you need for your purchase?"

Marianne thought, *He's a kind man. He does not use the word "shoes," and he is pretending that we are having a math lesson.* She said carefully, "I have fourpence here, and I have fivepence at home, but I'm saving it."

"If you want to buy something, as it is for a good cause, I am prepared to make you an indefinite loan. I am sure you will repay me as soon as you can. Do you think your parents would approve?"

"I think so. One day they'll come to England," said Marianne.

"I'll be happy to meet them," said Mr. Neame. "Here is sixpence."

"Thank you very much, Sir," said Marianne, and gave him one penny change. She handed over her money to the woman behind the shoe table. Marianne put her purchases in her schoolbag, and walked out of the gymnasium. She told herself she had nothing to feel ashamed of. Marianne ran all the way back to the house. The shoes might have sold if she'd waited till seven, and she did need them.

Gladys opened the door. "You're to wash your hands and brush your hair and go into the sitting room. There's someone to see you," she said.

Marianne knocked at the door.

"Come in, dear," said Aunt Vera.

Dear? She never calls me that. This must be someone pretty important.

"Mary Anne, this is Miss Morland. She has come from the Children's Refugee Committee to see how you've settled in with us."

Marianne said, "How do you do." She knew that no reply was expected.

Miss Morland said, "Well, Mary Anne, you *are* a lucky little girl to have found such a beautiful home. Mrs. Abercrombie Jones tells me your English is greatly improved. Is there anything you would like to ask me? No? Well, then, I really must go. I have one more visit to make today. The *Kindertransports* are arriving almost weekly now, Mrs. Abercrombie Jones. It's hard to place so many children. We are so grateful to people like you." Miss Morland stood up.

Marianne asked, "May I walk Miss Morland to the gate, Aunt Vera?"

Mrs. Abercrombie Jones hesitated, and then said too brightly, "Of course you may."

Marianne opened the front door. Perhaps she could talk to Miss Morland properly now.

Miss Morland said, "You were one of the early arrivals, weren't you? That must have been exciting."

Marianne said, "Yes. I am wondering about the orphans in Harwich and . . . and did the other children go to Jewish homes, or –"

Miss Morland interrupted her, "You all seem to be settling down nicely. That's what it's all about. Fitting in, and learning to be English girls and boys. Now I really have to go. Good-bye, dear."

Miss Morland shut the garden gate behind her, and walked briskly down the street.

Aunt Vera stood in the doorway.

"What were you and Miss Morland talking about, Mary Anne?"

"I asked her about something. It's not important."

Her chilblains started to itch. She'd changed into her almost-new shoes before going into the sitting room.

"Where did you get those shoes?" Aunt Vera uttered each word precisely.

"I bought them at the jumble sale," said Marianne.

"You did *what?*" Aunt Vera's voice went a notch higher. "Where did you get the money?"

"I had some left, and Mr. Neame lent me the rest. Aunt Vera, my shoes were too small."

"Do you realize what you've done, Mary Anne? You have made a spectacle of yourself. *Again*. Shamed me in front of everyone. People will say I am not taking proper care of you. You are an ungrateful, thoughtless girl. Why didn't you tell me? I will not tolerate this underhand behavior. Go to your room."

"I am sorry, Aunt Wera . . . Vera. I did not mean to be ungrateful. Are you going to send me away?" asked Marianne. She picked at her thumb.

"That possibility has crossed my mind. However, I accept your apology. You people do not behave in the same way as we do, I suppose," Aunt Vera said a little more calmly.

Marianne said again, "I am sorry to offend," and went upstairs.

Back in her room, Marianne hugged her bear, and looked out at the sky for a long time. Here, in this room at night, all the loneliness that she pushed away during the day settled around her like the fog that was so much a part of London.

"Be patient a little longer"

Marianne usually passed the postman on her way to school. Today he had a letter for her. "Good news from foreign parts I hope, Miss," he said.

Marianne tore off the corner of the envelope with the stamp on it and gave it to him for his little boy's stamp collection.

She read the letter in the playground and was almost late for registration. She got a bad mark for dictation, which she was usually good at, because she'd missed out two sentences.

After school she and Bridget walked to Bridget's house in silence. The girls sat in the kitchen, as they often did. Finally, Bridget spoke. "Why are you so upset?"

"What kind of mother sends letters like this?" Marianne said, spots of anger on her cheeks.

"Like what? Why don't you translate it?" Bridget asked.

Marianne read:

Hafenstrasse 26,
Düsseldorf, Deutschland

March 22, 1939

Dear Marianne,

Whenever one of your letters arrive, Opa, Oma, and I sit at the kitchen table, and I read it aloud several times. It's wonderful to hear of your good progress.

(Bridget rolled her eyes.)

"Well, I can't help it, you asked me to translate," said Marianne.

Oma and I are still struggling with the *th* sound. We pretend that we are English ladies in a tea shop and practice saying "the tea, the cake," but I don't think we're improving very much.

"That's nothing to get angry about," Bridget interrupted.

"Wait – you'll see," Marianne said.

Yesterday, when I came back from the consulate, I found a letter from England. Did you give someone my name, darling? A lady is looking for a cook / housekeeper. She asks if I am interested in the position.

Bridget jumped up and began singing and dancing "The Lambeth Walk," the dance that was sweeping England. She put her hand through Marianne's arm and they twirled round the kitchen.

Any time you're Lambeth way
Any evening, any day
You'll find us all doin' the Lambeth walk.

Everything's free and easy.
Do as you darn well pleasey.

"If we could 'do as we darn well pleasey,' everything'd be alright. Stop it, Bridget. I haven't finished yet."

"Sorry." Bridget sat down and nibbled a biscuit.

Marianne continued:

I asked Opa's friend to translate for me to make sure that I understood properly. The lady writes that her mother lives in a country village outside Farnham. She is elderly and needs someone to take charge of the household. Naturally I wrote back at once and told her this sounded a perfect situation for me and I would let her know as soon as possible. I'm trying to contact David to ask his advice.

Since you left, restrictions have been tightened. Jews may no longer use the town library, drive cars, own radios, telephones, or pets, and may shop for only one hour a day. How will Oma and Opa manage without me? If I come, I may bring only one suitcase. I'd arrive with nothing, like a beggar. Yes, you did it too, but you are a child. How will I be able to send for Oma and Opa? It's too big a decision to make overnight. Try to understand, darling, and be patient a little longer.

"Why must I be the one to understand?" said Marianne. "It's about time someone remembered me. What's she waiting for – a written invitation from the king?" Marianne stopped, too angry and upset to continue.

Bridget looked down at her plate. She crumbled her biscuit.

"I don't believe she's saying these things. She promised. And now she's making all these excuses." Marianne's voice trembled.

Bridget looked up. "She can't just pack a bag and hop on a train."

"Why not? If she says yes, then she'll get her visa, and come, and I'll have a mother again, like everyone else." Marianne was close to tears.

"Not everyone. There's a girl in my class at school whose mother died last year," said Bridget.

"Of natural causes, not on purpose. There's going to be a war. Don't you ever look at the news headlines? Even Uncle Geoffrey mumbles, 'Bound to be a war.' Everyone will be killed. My father in Prague, my mother and grandparents in Germany, my aunt and uncle and cousin in Holland. They'll all die and I'll be left alone."

"You're being melodramatic, Mary Anne. You know you're exaggerating," said Bridget.

77

"And you know *nothing!*" Marianne was almost shouting.

Dr. O'Malley came into the kitchen. "I've got ten minutes before my next patient. I was looking for your mother to make me a cup of tea."

"Ma's shopping. I'll make it," said Bridget.

"That's my good girl," said her father.

Marianne burst into tears. *It's not fair – why don't I have a father to make tea for?* "I'm sorry, I have to go," said Marianne, pushing back her chair.

"Sit down, Mary Anne," said Dr. O'Malley, "you'll ruin my reputation. People will say, 'That Dr. O'Malley must be an awful bad doctor. Did you see that pretty little girl with the light brown hair leave the surgery crying?' Pour us all a cup of tea, Bridget, my love."

So they all had cups of tea and ate ginger biscuits.

"Good gracious, look at the time. Mrs. Briggs will be waiting, and complaining. 'I haven't got all day, Doctor dear,' she'll say." Dr. O'Malley tweaked Bridget's curls, smiled at Marianne, and was gone.

"Sorry, Bridget," Marianne mumbled, ashamed.

"It's that loudmouthed Hitler who should be sorry, messing up people's lives. I heard Pa say that the world hasn't got a chance till we get rid of the fascist swine."

"Bridget O'Malley, don't let your mother hear you use words like that," said Marianne.

"I'm only quoting what my father said. Listen, Mary Anne, can I tell you something?"

"You're going to anyway," said Marianne.

"I think your mum is right to try and talk to your father. I mean, she can't just disappear. My mother doesn't even buy a hat without asking Pa's advice," Bridget said.

"But she doesn't know where he is. And with the Nazis in Prague, how can she talk to him?" Marianne tried to keep her voice steady.

"They're bound to have friends who can smuggle messages. Well, it's only polite to discuss something big like going to England. And then there's your grandparents. I expect she needs a bit of time to prepare them, or something. You know what old people are like," said Bridget.

"I never even got a chance to say good-bye to Opa and Oma," said Marianne.

Bridget replied, "That's the way it is. We're children. No one asks us what we want to do. Don't you feel proud that your idea worked? You're eleven years old and you got your mother a job! Cheer up – let's have a game of cards. What about Old Maid?"

"Better not. I can't be late for tea. I never thought I'd be at Aunt Vera's this long. I really thought Mutti would come over in a couple of weeks."

"Stay a bit longer," coaxed Bridget.

"I can't. I've got to copy out my composition for the head-mistress. Wonder why she wants to see it?"

"Probably wants to show off the brilliance of her star German pupil to the school inspector," said Bridget.

"One, I'm the only so-called German pupil in the school, and two, don't call me that. I don't call you Irish."

Bridget opened the front door for Marianne, and suddenly hugged her. "Now it's only because I'm Irish I'm doing that. Those cold fishes, the English, would shake hands and they're not too keen on doing that, either. Good-bye, Miss Marianne Kohn," Bridget said, pronouncing her name the German way. "I'll see you tomorrow."

"Sure you will," said Marianne in her best imitation of an Irish brogue.

On the way home, every time she avoided stepping on a line on the pavement, she said, "Mother's coming." By the time she reached her corner, it had turned into a refrain: "Mother's coming, Mother's coming, Mother's coming."

· 13 ·

"Skolership"

After tea, Marianne copied out her composition, careful to correct every word that she'd misspelt. There weren't many red sp. signs in the margin. "Silence" was a tricky one; she'd always thought it was spelled with two s's. That was the trouble with English – there were so many rules and just when you thought you'd learnt them all, there'd be an exception. Like receive – i before e except after c. It'd be so much easier to write "recieve."

Miss Martin hadn't given them a choice of topic as she usually did. She'd said, "Sometimes people have to write about a subject, even if it's difficult." But everyone liked doing this one.

When Miss Martin handed Marianne's composition back to her, she'd given her an A-, and told her to copy it neatly, and hand it in to the office next day.

It was late before she'd finished. She read it over carefully one more time:

18 March, 1939

HOME
by Marianne Kohn

The dictionary says home is the place where you live. I disagree. Home is the place where your parents are.

England is a nice country, but it is not my home.

My name, my face, my clothes, my speech are all from somewhere else. They make me different.

For three and one-half months, I've lived in this house. I eat good food, sleep in a bed in a room only for me.

Still I do not fit. I am a stranger.

Everything is cold. Winter is cold, I know – this cold is the cold I feel without my parents.

A home is where people want you to stay, not from duty. Where they like you, also if you make mistakes.

In a home someone tells you, "Goodnight, sleep well."

Here no one sees when I am sad. I am not family, not a poor relation.

I am "our little refugee."

I will never forget the first days. The words I cannot understand. The long silence when no one speaks to me.

I think it is a bad dream. Tomorrow I will wake up in my own bed.

I remember I feel hungry, and when food comes, I cannot eat because the pain in my heart is so big.

Home is where people love you, and where you love them too.

The end.

Marianne's last thought before going to sleep was of her parents. Ten minutes was all the time Mutti had given her to decide whether she'd go to England. Even then she'd known she'd have to leave. It wasn't a real choice. She hoped Mutti would remember that and realize that *she* didn't have one either.

Next morning, before Assembly, Marianne handed in her composition. Two days later, a prefect knocked at the classroom door, and said, "The headmistress says will you please excuse Mary Anne Kohn. She wants to see her right away in her study."

"Thank you, Millie. Run along, Mary Anne."

Marianne walked down the corridor, smoothing her hair before she knocked on the door marked HEADMISTRESS.

"Come in, Mary Anne, and pull up that chair. That's right."

Opposite the headmistress, sitting in the visitor's chair, was Aunt Vera.

Whatever have I done? Am I in trouble? She couldn't think of anything serious enough for Aunt Vera to be summoned to see the headmistress. *Has something happened to my parents?*

"Don't look so worried, dear," said Miss Barton.

Easy to say. She knew Aunt Vera. She looked her least approachable, and her face was flushed as though she was angry.

"I expect you are surprised to see Mrs. Abercrombie Jones here in the middle of the day."

"Yes, Miss Barton. Good morning, Aunt Vera."

"An opportunity has come Mary Anne's way, Mrs. Abercrombie Jones, which requires a guardian's consent." Miss Barton smiled at Aunt Vera, who sort of smiled back. "If Mary Anne had arrived earlier in this country, she would have sat the scholarship exam with her class. As it is, she has caught up remarkably well and has been offered a free place at St. John's Grammar School for Girls. Well done, my dear. Miss Lacey, the headmistress there, suggests that Mary Anne start school after the Easter holidays. The scholarship includes books, fees, and an allowance toward school uniforms. It would be a pity to deny her such an opportunity. So many more avenues will open up – even university will be within her reach from grammar school. I do hope, Mrs. Abercrombie Jones, you will permit Mary Anne to accept the award."

Marianne held her breath. *Surely Aunt Vera won't say no?* It would be something for Aunt Vera to boast about to her friends: "Look how our little refugee has progressed."

Marianne looked down at the Indian carpet, studying the red and brown design as if her life depended on her memorizing the pattern. She would not let Aunt Vera see how much this meant to her.

Aunt Vera cleared her throat. "I shall of course discuss the matter with my husband. I cannot possibly give you an immediate answer, Miss Barton. It is a very kind gesture; however, I feel . . . *we* feel that Mary Anne must begin to learn something that will enable her to earn her living as soon as possible. Most girls leave school at fourteen. Mary Anne should not be pampered because she is a refugee."

Miss Barton said, "Mary Anne's achievement does you and your husband great credit. That will be all, Mary Anne. You may return to class."

Marianne carefully replaced her chair against the wall. "Thank you, Miss Barton. Good-bye, Aunt Vera."

There, I've managed to say the name correctly for once. Surely that will count for something?

Outside the headmistress' study, the secretary smiled at her, and asked, "Everything alright, dear?"

"Yes, thank you."

Marianne didn't know how she could sit through history class, or the next five minutes, without telling Bridget her news. If only Aunt Vera could be persuaded to let her go to St. John's. She wouldn't be fourteen for over two years, and not even twelve till May. Lots could happen in that time. She didn't want to have to live and work in other people's houses like Miriam and her friend. She wanted to have a choice.

Class had begun. Marianne apologized for being late and sat down. Bridget passed her a note. "What did you do? Are you in trouble?"

Marianne wrote: "I got a skolership to your grammar school." She dropped the note between their desks.

"Stand up, Mary Anne Kohn," thundered Mr. Stevens. "Bring me that note."

"Pardon?" Marianne tried to push it under her desk with the toe of her shoe. Beside her, Bridget was trying to smother her laughter.

"I am sure you are perfectly able to understand a simple request. Bring me that note."

"Yes, Sir." Marianne picked up the piece of paper and gave it to Mr. Stevens. He read it without comment.

"Return to your desk. I trust, Bridget, that you have recovered from your fit of apoplexy. You will both stay after school and write five hundred times: 'I must pay attention in class.' Congratulations, Mary Anne. Oh, and write the word 'scholarship' correctly twenty-five times."

Marianne smiled at Mr. Stevens, thinking him the nicest teacher in the whole school. She decided to send Mutti a copy of the composition – it might help persuade her to come to England.

· 14 ·

Waiting for the War

Nothing more had been said to Marianne about St. John's Grammar School for Girls, except one Sunday after church, when the vicar said, "I hear our little protégée has won a scholarship, Mrs. Abercrombie Jones."

Aunt Vera smiled, but said nothing.

"Must be doing something right, wouldn't you say, Vicar?" said Uncle Geoffrey, and laughed, but Marianne had not known she was going for certain until she was measured for her uniform. It was like having an early birthday present – the only one this year, except for the box of chocolates Bridget had given her.

By June the weather had turned hot, and Marianne and Bridget were sprawled on the grass at the edge of the playing field.

"We're bound to be at war soon. It's exciting in a way, isn't it?" said Bridget. "I don't mean the killing, but being evacuated on our own, not knowing where we're going to end up. We'll have fun, Mary Anne. Let's tell everyone we refuse to be separated, that my mother says we have to stay together." Bridget rolled over on her back, shielding her eyes with her straw hat.

Marianne shivered in spite of the heat. The very thought of another railway station and a train journey made her feel sick and afraid.

Everyone seemed to be almost looking forward to the war. *Funny how quickly people get used to something terrible.*

They watched the sausage-shaped silver barrage balloons overhead. They'd been told that the balloons would confuse the German planes when they came, so they'd just turn back. Marianne was afraid that Marshall Goering, shaped like a balloon himself in his gold-braided uniform, would find a way to get the planes through and bomb them all. *If there's nothing to worry about, why are shelters being built, ditches dug, and sandbags filled? And why are we going to be sent away?*

The whistle blew. Lunch hour was over. Bridget and Marianne ran so as not to be late for geography. Marianne liked this class. It was soothing coloring maps of Europe, and outlining the different countries in black ink. She placed a red dot for the capital of each country, and printed the name beside it.

When she came to Czechoslovakia, a tear fell on Prague, so that it looked as if tiny rivers branched out of the city. She dried the smudge with a piece of blotting paper. It didn't look too bad. She was always crying lately. She hated being such a baby.

Whenever she dusted the dining room, she took a long time with the glass decanter set that Uncle Geoffrey had said came from Prague. Liking the idea of touching something from the country which harbored her father, her eyes filled with tears every time.

Aunt Vera noticed last week. "What's the matter, Mary Anne? Big girls of twelve don't cry for no reason," she said.

"I'm getting a cold, Aunt Vera. My eyes are watering, that's all."

Marianne didn't feel like confiding that she hadn't seen her father since last November, and then for only a short time. She was beginning to confuse him with Leslie Howard, the film star. She'd seen him in her first English film, *The Scarlet Pimpernel*. It was all about saving the aristocracy from the guillotine in the French Revolution. Leslie Howard had escaped his pursuers over and over again. She'd watched in agony, fearing each time would be his last. Perhaps her father would manage to escape, too.

Miss Beasley rapped on the table. "Put your work on my desk, girls, and line up in single file to go to the gymnasium. Bring your gas masks. No talking, please."

Gas mask drill was worse than eating porridge on mornings when Gladys had quarreled with her fiancé. On those days the porridge was always lumpy or scorched.

Marianne didn't know anyone who liked wearing a gas mask, even though the drill meant they sometimes got out of classes like math.

"Hold you breath, girls, jut out your chin, hold the straps, and now put them back over your head," said the gym teacher.

What they didn't warn you about was the way your ears roared, as though you were on the deck of a ship in a howling gale when you let out your breath, or about the stench of new rubber. You had to keep the mask on for at least ten minutes. Marianne had found a way to keep the procedure bearable. She recited the last two lines of Walter de la Mare's poem "Five Eyes." Her English teacher said it would help her pronunciation:

> Out come his cats all grey with meal –
> Jekkel, and Jessup, and one-eyed Jill.

By the time she'd remembered to make the hard *J* sound three times in a row, it'd be time to pull off the gas mask. All the girls looked the same when they emerged from the masks – red and perspiring – and some had tears in their eyes because they hated wearing the masks so much.

Talk of war was everywhere. Uncle Geoffrey's office was going to be evacuated to Torquay any day, right away from London. Aunt Vera had been up to the little seaside town to speak to real estate agents.

Every morning Marianne would rush downstairs to see if there was a letter for her. There was a slot at the front door for the postman to put the letters through. But Gladys had usually picked the post up before she could get to it, and put it beside Uncle Geoffrey's plate, and then she'd have to wait till he gave it to her after he'd finished his breakfast.

At last one morning a letter arrived. Marianne was almost afraid to open it.

25 June, 1939

Dear Marianne,

I'm all packed up and just waiting for one more signature on my exit visa. I can't think what the holdup is. I hope it won't take very much longer. Someone must be playing a game of cat and mouse with us. Opa and Oma send their love to you and are happy that you and I will be together again soon.

Oma has baked gingersnaps for you, and I will bring a loaf of dark rye bread. All that white flour can't be good for you.

Your glass animals are safely stored in the attic, and Opa says he will guard them with his life. How I've missed you, Marianne.

Lots of love from us all,
Mutti

The summer holidays would be starting in July, and she and her mother would have till the middle of September before school began again. *Will Mutti recognize me?* She'd grown a lot, nearly two inches. She wasn't a little girl anymore. She'd help her mother, look after her. It would be lovely to sit down together, the way they used to, both of them drinking coffee, and filling in all the gaps of their time apart. Letters were never enough.

The days passed – still there was no news of her mother's arrival.

The summer holidays began, and a letter was sent to each girl's home outlining instructions to follow if war was declared before the start of the new term.

Still no news from Mutti. *Something must have happened. Supposing Mutti has been arrested?*

The nightmare began again. It was always the same one. She was back in Germany. She watched her mother coming down the street, walking arm in arm with her grandmother towards her grandparents' house. A car stopped beside them. Soldiers pulled them into the car. Marianne called out. They didn't see or hear her. The car roared away. She was left alone in the empty street.

That was the moment Marianne woke up, and only the reality of holding her bear and humming their familiar lullaby gave her enough courage to go back to sleep.

· 15 ·

"We'll go together"

The sun shone every day. It should have been a perfect summer, but it wasn't. Marianne waited for news of her mother's arrival, and the country waited for war. In Parliament, Mr. Chamberlain, the prime minister of England, said that England would stand by Poland, if she was attacked by Hitler.

Marianne helped Gladys hem blackout curtains for all the windows. Not even a sliver of light was allowed to show through.

Uncle Geoffrey stored cans of petrol in the garage. "That's the first thing that will be rationed when war comes," he said.

Aunt Vera, Gladys, and Marianne were putting away vast amounts of tinned food in the pantry. "I have no intention of running short of food if there is a siege. How many tins of fruit do we have now, Gladys?" Aunt Vera said.

"One dozen tins of peaches, six large tins of pears, and one dozen tins of fruit salad, Madam." Gladys spoke from the top of the stepladder in the pantry. Marianne had scrubbed all the shelves earlier.

"Mary Anne, I want you to run down to Brown's, and ask for six tins of pineapple chunks – large tins. Have him charge my account. Oh, and ask him to deliver another six tins of corned beef. Is there anything else, Gladys?"

"It wouldn't hurt to have some jars of jam and marmalade, Madam. It might be hard to get sugar later on to make jam."

"Very well. Mary Anne, add six jars of marmalade and four jars of strawberry jam. Can you remember all that?"

"Yes, Aunt Vera."

How long do they think the war is going to last? And "siege," doesn't that mean holding out against the invader? If the invader is Hitler, can they hold out? Marianne ran all the way to the greengrocer at the corner of the High Street.

It was quite embarrassing asking for so much food. Mr. Brown raised an eyebrow. He probably thought that Aunt Vera was being greedy. On the way back, Marianne saw that someone had chalked a slogan on the side of the store: YESTERDAY VIENNA AND PRAGUE, TOMORROW WARSAW AND LONDON.

It was true. Marianne tried to think of logical explanations for her mother's silence. The only bearable one was that her mother was trying to surprise her.

Uncle Geoffrey kept the government pamphlets, which arrived almost daily, in a folder on the sideboard: WHAT TO DO IN AN AIR RAID and IF THE INVADER COMES, along with warnings about always carrying your gas mask.

One day a man came to school, and talked about what happened in the 1914–1918 war, and showed them gruesome
pictures about the effects of mustard gas. Some of the girls had
looked at Marianne as if she were personally responsible. She
remembered the day she had blurted out, "My father fought in
the last war." Hilary, who was always making catty remarks, said
in that snobbish voice of hers, "On whose side, my dear?" Only
the bell at the end of recess had saved her having to answer.

There'd been notices about schoolchildren being evacuated to
the countryside, and lists of things to bring. They practiced and
practiced how to behave on "the day."

Perfect sunshine continued right through the summer holidays.

"Ma says she thinks my last year's bathing suit will fit you. You
do know how to swim, don't you?" Bridget handed Marianne a
bright blue shirred elastic suit.

Marianne remembered the last time she'd gone to the swim-
ming baths in Berlin. There was a large notice beside the booth
where you paid for your entrance fee. It said: JEWS AND DOGS
NOT ADMITTED.

Her mother had taken her hand and they'd walked past.
She'd said, "Another time, perhaps, darling." Now here she was
doing all those things that she'd missed so much. The knowledge that her mother couldn't share this golden summer nagged
at her, making her feel guilty at having fun. The thought kept

returning like a wasp that came back even after you'd swatted it away.

"I don't believe there's going to be a war. It's much too hot, who'd want to fight?" Bridget said, fanning herself with the copy of *Film Fun* she'd been reading.

The girls finished their sandwiches. They ate in Bridget's garden, or in the park, most afternoons.

"Your Anderson shelter looks pretty. I like the flowerpots your mother arranged at the side. Kind of like a rockery, with all that greenery on top. Uncle Geoffrey told us, 'I refuse to ruin my lawn or disturb my roses for that tin contraption. We will use the cupboard under the stairs if there is any danger from bombs.' Gladys and I had to clear out the cupboard. I don't know how I'm going to sit in that cubbyhole breathing in smoke from Uncle Geoffrey's pipe and listening to Aunt Vera complaining about everything."

"The Anderson smells damp already, and there's slugs. Think of stepping on them in the dark – ugh! Let's hope there'll never be an air raid," said Bridget, sharing her Milky Way bar with Marianne.

On August 29, the school recalled the girls for a final evacuation dress rehearsal. The headmistress told them to keep their rucksacks and bags packed, as they might have to leave at any moment. They were told to bring a stamped addressed card so they could write their parents as soon as they knew their new addresses. Even the teachers had no idea where they were going.

Bridget smiled at Marianne, who deliberately pretended not to see. She hated being pitied because she had no parents to send information to. The moment war broke out, she'd be cut off from her family forever. She really would be an orphan.

On the way home from school, Bridget and Marianne stopped to watch the swans in Regent's Park. "What will happen to them in an air raid, do you think?" Marianne asked.

"They'll hide under the little bridge, or in the rushes, I expect. They'll be alright. Stop worrying so much, Mary Anne."

"Can't help it. Bridget, I've had the same dream two nights in a row."

"You mean a nightmare?"

"No, this time it's a good dream. I'm standing on the platform at the station – a train's just come in. The guard opens the carriage door and my mother comes down the steps, and she's holding out her arms to me. It means she's coming, doesn't it?"

"Or that the letter's on its way saying when she's going to arrive. Or, listen, Mary Anne, it may mean that you want it to happen so much. . . ."

"You mean wishful thinking, don't you? It isn't only that, I won't believe that. I'm going to the station every single day to wait for her."

"Every day?"

"I have to go. I'll tell you something I haven't told anyone. I went to Liverpool Street Station once before. I mean, I never actually got there. I turned back. It was after I arrived. I was so lonely. Then I got scared."

"Of what? What did you think could happen?"

"I don't know exactly. I couldn't speak much English, and it reminded me of leaving Berlin. There was no point in going anyway. I wouldn't have known anyone. I'm going to try again. I know that if I do this, she'll be there."

Bridget said, "I'll call for you in the morning. Wait for me. We'll go together the first time. You don't have to go alone."

Next morning the household was in a small uproar. Marianne could tell Gladys was upset by the way she put down the plates. She'd learnt to watch for danger signals even before she could speak English properly. It was important to do that when you lived in someone else's home.

Aunt Vera was speaking in her highest voice and her cheeks were flushed as though she'd put on too much rouge. "I'm afraid you'll have to manage, Gladys. I'm sorry about your afternoon off, but it can't be helped. We're almost at war. I shall catch the 9:10 A.M. to Torquay. Mr. Abercrombie Jones thinks he has found a flat that might do for us while his office is relocated. Please keep the wireless on, in case of any announcements."

"Do you mean about trains to Torquay, Aunt Vera?" Marianne asked.

"Are you being impertinent, or is this another example of your German sense of humor?"

Marianne met Aunt Vera's eyes. It was hard not to answer back. There was no point in aggravating Aunt Vera when she was in this mood. "I'm sorry, Aunt Vera, I did not understand what you meant," Marianne said politely.

Mrs. Abercrombie Jones turned to Gladys, who was wiping the table. "There may be a government announcement concerning the evacuation, or a declaration of war at any moment. Mary Anne, give your room a thorough cleaning and polish the floor, please. Everything must be ready." Aunt Vera swept out of the room.

Ready for what? Do invaders care if the floors are shiny?

There was a knock on the scullery door.

"My hands are soapy," said Gladys.

Marianne opened the door.

"Bridget, I was waiting for you. I'll get my blazer and tell Gladys we'll be gone the rest of the day."

"No, don't. I can't stay. I have to go straight back home, but first I've got to tell you something. Come out a minute." Bridget looked pale. Her eyes were red, as though she'd been crying.

Marianne shut the door behind them, and they crossed the street and walked down Wellington Road towards the park. "What happened?" Marianne asked. "Aren't you allowed to come to the station?"

"Much worse than that." Bridget blew her nose. "I'm leaving for Canada. Uncle John sent a telegram from Montreal. It said: SEND BRIDGET IMMEDIATELY. Then Pa telephoned and it's all arranged – I'm going."

"It's awfully far away," said Marianne.

"I begged Pa," said Bridget. "I told him I wanted to go with the school, that we wanted to stay together. I said, 'I'm not a baby – I'm entitled to my opinion,' and Pa slammed his fist on the table and said, 'The subject is not up for discussion. John is my elder brother. You will be safe with him.' Then he stormed out."

"Didn't your mother say anything?" Marianne asked, hoping that somehow it would end happily, that somehow they wouldn't be parted.

"Naturally, she took Pa's side. She said it's important to be with your own flesh and blood, and how Canada was a wonderful country, and about the food and fresh air, and how it wouldn't be for long. You know the kind of things parents say."

"When are you leaving?" Marianne asked very quietly, trying not to show how upset she was.

"The boat sails tomorrow," said Bridget. "I have to break my promise. Sorry."

"It's not your fault. I understand," said Marianne.

They walked back without talking anymore. When they reached the corner of Circus Road, Bridget handed her a note. "Here is my address in Canada. I wrote it out for you. Tell me everything that happens to you and your parents, and oh, Mary Anne, I wish you were coming with me and let's always stay friends."

They hugged good-bye.

When Marianne got back, she went up to her bedroom and closed the door quietly. Then she threw herself on her bed and cried and cried.

It was late before she finished cleaning her room, too late to go to the station.

· 16 ·

"Remember me"

Marianne got up very early next morning. She scribbled a note to Gladys: "I'll be back tonight, something I must do."

Luckily Gladys was still talking to the milkman on the front steps, so she didn't need to explain. She grabbed a couple of apples and put them in her blazer pocket. Closing the door carefully behind her, she ran to catch the bus that would take her to her mother.

The number eleven stopped at the end of the High Street. Marianne held tightly to the wooden railings so as not to lose her balance as she climbed to the top of the bus. The penny halfpenny ride took her through the heart of London. Marianne knew that the moment war was declared, the lights of all the neon signs in Piccadilly Circus, advertising BOVRIL, SCHWEPPES, the latest films, would be blacked out. She couldn't imagine the whole city in darkness.

The statue of the little boy Eros had sandbags around the base. They were piled up around Nelson's Column in Trafalgar Square, too.

The bus went down Threadneedle Street. Marianne visualized all the tailors and seamstresses who had worked and lived here over the centuries, for whom the street had been named. She was sure there were immigrants like her among them. Now they were passing St. Paul's Cathedral – the spires seemed to touch the sky.

The conductor rang the bell. "Liverpool Street Station, next stop."

Marianne hurried down the steps of the bus. The station was just as she remembered it: the tall wrought-iron gates next to the taxi ramp, the newsboys brandishing their papers, the shining glass roof. Today the sun glared through. It was too hot to wear a blazer. Marianne suddenly realized she could understand all the announcements. She did not even have to translate the words first.

She asked a porter, "Which platform for the boat train from Harwich, please?"

"Platform five, ducks, due in three minutes," he said.

A boy shouted a news headline: HITLER SEEKS ENGLISH GERMAN FRIENDSHIP.

A soldier leaning against a pillar said, "Not bloody likely." And stubbed out his cigarette, grinding it into the floor.

Marianne followed a large woman, her husband, and two children onto platform five. The train was just coming in. The ticket collector must have thought she belonged to the family – he didn't ask to see her platform ticket. She hadn't bought one. She was trying to save money for when her mother arrived.

The platform was packed with friends, families, and officials to greet the new arrivals. They surged forward as the compartments emptied. Snatches of Polish, French, German, and Czech floated in the air.

Marianne searched the faces of the passengers. There were students with bulging rucksacks, businessmen wearing Homburg hats and carrying briefcases, tired-looking men and women, some wearing fur coats in spite of the heat. They looked pale and lost standing among their luggage, as though waiting to be rescued.

A woman in a navy coat and hat stood by an open carriage door, her back to Marianne.

She is *here.* "Mutti!" Marianne ran forward.

The woman turned round slowly, and looked straight at Marianne. Then she raised her hand and waved and smiled, and a man moved out of the crowd towards her. He put out his arms and lifted a little girl from the steps of the carriage. The woman clung to his arm and they walked very close together towards the exit.

Marianne felt dizzy for a moment, as though she were going to faint.

A group of about forty children, labels round their necks, filed neatly past Marianne – not talking, trying to be brave.

Is that what I looked like when I came? Marianne wanted to call out "Don't be afraid," but her mouth felt too dry to speak and she didn't know whether to say it in English or German. She pulled out one of her apples and gave it to a small boy, trailing at the end of the line. He reminded her of Bernard.

Marianne waited until four o'clock. Many other trains arrived during that long hot day.

A train guard holding a green flag asked, "Are you waiting for someone?"

"I'm meeting my mother; she's coming from Harwich."

"That was the last boat train for today," the official said.

"Thank you, Sir." Numbly, Marianne walked away and out of the station.

On the way home on the bus, all Marianne could think was, *She isn't coming. Not today, not ever.*

When she got in, Gladys said, "Where've you *been?* The announcement came." Then she looked at Marianne and said, "You look in a daze. Did you hear what I said? It was on the wireless. You're being evacuated tomorrow. You have to be at school at 6:30 A.M. sharp. Hurry up now and eat your tea, then put your things together. I'll make you cheese and tomato sandwiches for the journey, shall I?"

"Thank you, Gladys," said Marianne. She slumped down on the kitchen chair.

"Don't slump, Marianne. You're such a pretty girl." Marianne looked up. Her mother's voice was as clear as if she were sitting beside her. There was the voice again. "You mean you haven't eaten all day? Drink your milk at once, please. You need your strength for the journey." Marianne drank her milk to the last drop without stopping. She ate three slices of bread and goose-berry jam, and a piece of sultana cake.

Gladys said, "Mrs. Abercrombie Jones rang up. She can't get back till after you leave. She said to give you half a crown from the housekeeping." She slid a coin across the table. "They're closing up the house and staying in Torquay till all this is over."

"But war hasn't started yet. There's got to be time," Marianne said agonizingly, hoping her mother could still reach her.

"Time for what? You've been out too long in the sun. I give it three days at most. Friday, tomorrow, first of September. You'll see."

Marianne stood and hung up her blazer. Her fingers touched the gold school crest on the pocket. IN GOD WE TRUST. There was nothing she could do to stop the war coming. Lots of people would be separated from one another; she wasn't the only one – Bridget and her family, Mutti and Vati, thousands of children and their parents. She'd better start acting her age, be stronger, and not feel sorry for herself all the time. She'd begin right this minute. *I'll be someone my parents can be proud of, so I'll have nothing to be ashamed of after the war's over. Wars don't last forever. Mutti could still get here.*

"What's going to happen to you, Gladys? Are you getting married now?" Marianne asked.

"Not till it's all over. I'll look for war work. There'll be plenty of jobs going. Even the milkman's joining the army. He told me this morning. I always fancied working on the buses. A clippie, you know. Clipping tickets. Now you go up to bed. You look done in," Gladys said kindly.

"Thank you, Gladys, and for all the good meals and everything. Goodnight."

Marianne didn't have much to pack; she'd done most of it.
Only last-minute things were left. She washed out her under-
clothes and hung them out of the window, so that they'd be dry
by morning. She checked the room to make sure she hadn't forgotten anything. She wasn't glad or sorry to leave. It was just a
room she'd been lent. It had never really felt like her own.

Before she went to bed, she wrote a note to Mr. and Mrs.
Abercrombie Jones to leave on the hall table in the morning:

31 August, 1939

Dear Aunt Vera and Uncle Geoffrey,

    Thank you for taking me into your home, and for the
half crown. I have learnt a lot here. I am grateful.

Yours sincerely,
Marianne Kohn

She read it over. Aunt Vera and Uncle Geoffrey had done the
best they could. They didn't know about children, and they
thought being foreign was something to be got over, like measles.
They probably wouldn't see each other again.

In the morning, she shook hands with Gladys. "Thank you,
Gladys. One day I might ride on your bus. I hope so."

"Good luck, Mary Anne." Gladys patted Marianne's shoulder
awkwardly, and handed her a big lunch bag.

On the way to school the postman stopped her. "Off to the country, are you? My lad's going too. You've got a card today. Glad I didn't miss you." He rummaged in his bag and handed Marianne a plain white card. It was written in pencil, which had faded a bit. It said:

Dear Marianne,
    I love you. Remember me.

                                                            Vati

Marianne put the card in her shoulder bag. Her father seemed very close to her at that moment. It felt almost as if he were walking beside her, reminding her to be brave.

"Postie," Marianne called. "Thank you *very* much. Good-bye."

Her suitcase felt much lighter. She wished she could tell Bridget she'd heard from her father.

· 17 ·

Evacuation

It was strange being in the school's assembly hall so early. Every girl's eyes were riveted on the headmistress. Miss Lacey led the school in prayers for a safe journey, then she said: "The next time we talk to one another as a school, we will be in a strange hall, in someone else's building. None of us know when we will be back here in St. John's, or even if our school will still be standing after the war. We are setting off on the biggest adventure of our lives, and like our brave soldiers, sailors, and airmen, we do not know where we are going or what awaits us. We do know that homes will be provided for us in places of safety.

"I am proud that our school is part of the greatest exodus from the city that has ever happened. Be good ambassadors wherever you go, so that the generous people who are opening their homes to us will be glad that they have done so."

The girls filed back to their classrooms in total silence to the strains of the organ playing "Land of Hope and Glory." The music had never sounded more eloquent.

When Miss Barry handed out luggage labels, Marianne's hand shook. It was only nine months since she had worn one of those. Everyone in class had to print their names, and that of their school on one. Then they tied the labels round their necks with bits of string. A girl put up her hand and said, "We're not likely to forget our names. Do we have to wear these?"

"Yes. In the event of an accident, that label may be an important means of identification," said Miss Barry.

No one spoke another word after that.

Miss Barry smiled and said, "Time to read one more chapter." She opened *The Railway Children* and continued reading to the class. They'd reached the part where the rock falls on the railway line, and Peter, Bobbie, and Phyllis have to find a way to stop the 11:29 A.M. train from hurtling off the track.

The bell rang.

"That means the buses are here," said Miss Barry. "I'll take the book with me and once school recommences after the holidays and we are settled in our new classroom, I shall finish the story. You may line up and walk to the gates, and remember Miss Lacey's words: 'Be good ambassadors wherever you go' . . . and don't forget to bring your gas masks!"

Outside the gates of the playground, a line of buses was waiting. Marianne saw that someone had written GOOD-BYE HITLER in chalk, on the side of one.

Now that Bridget was on her way to Canada, Marianne didn't have anyone to sit with. The only empty seat was beside Hilary, whose regular partner had been sent to relatives in the country. Hilary edged as far away from Marianne as she could.

When they got to Paddington Station, the foreground was packed with single and double-decker buses. Inside, there were thousands of schoolchildren from all over London, mothers with toddlers, also going to the country, and volunteers, who handed out slabs of chocolate, cups of tea, and kind words for everyone.

The hardest part for Marianne was seeing all the mothers, and even some fathers, shouting advice, tying hair ribbons, and giving last-minute hugs.

Miss Barry had counted their class twice, making sure no one was missing, and at last it was time to board. They were allocated compartments in alphabetical order, so even if Bridget had been here, she and Marianne might not have sat together.

Once the girls were settled, Miss Barry came round and gave them each a packet of barley sugar. "The best cure for travel sickness I know," she said, and left them to say their good-byes. Marianne sat in her seat trying not to mind, or look as if she minded, that she had no one to wave to. She must be the only girl on the train without a relative on the platform. She was glad when the guard blew the whistle at last and the engine began to move.

Miss Barry came in again. "Now I'm just three compartments away, and I'll be in every half hour to check if you're alright," she said.

Celia was crying quietly in her corner seat. "I wish I hadn't come," she sobbed.

Miss Barry said briskly, "We've scarcely left the station, and remember, ambassadors don't cry."

"When will we get to wherever we're going, Miss Barry?" Jane asked.

"I have no idea, Jane, but I suspect we have a long journey ahead, so make yourself comfortable and enjoy the scenery."

The train was smartly painted in blue with gold lettering and inside, it was comfortable. The seats were padded; there were even armrests.

Miss Barry had told them that today all the railways were reserved for the great evacuation, and no one else could travel. It made it seem like a real adventure.

The girls sang: "Ten green bottles hanging on the wall/ There were ten in the bed and the little one said, 'Roll over.'" They sang the First World War song "It's a Long Way to Tipperary," and "Daisy, Daisy, give me your answer do!" They waved to people standing at railway crossings, and to children sitting on stiles. They played "I Spy," and saw towns change to villages and farms. All the stations they passed through had the names covered up, so that any enemy spies wouldn't know where the children were being taken. Then they divided themselves up into teams and kept count of animals. Marianne's team won by one sheep.

The train stopped often. The girls grew restless. Miss Barry let them go in two's to the guards' van, where there was a supply of drinking water in a big churn.

Lucy came back and said, "We're in Wales."

"How do you know?" Jane asked.

"Because the guard said, 'We're coming into Aberdare,' and then he said, 'Not a word, mind.' I happen to know Aberdare is in Wales because we had a holiday there once."

Celia said, "Wales is a foreign country. The Welsh don't even speak English, or not much." And she started crying again.

Marianne wondered if Welsh was harder to learn than English.

Jane said, "What fun if they can't understand what we're saying."

Marianne could have told them it wasn't any fun at all, but decided it wasn't the right moment.

The landscape, which had been a mixture of green hills and little stone cottages, began to change. Now the train plunged into a valley scarred with huge black coal tips, like mountains.

Eight hours after they'd left London, the train drew up into a small station and the girls overflowed onto the narrow gray platform. Buses were waiting for them. The bus driver said, "A friendly little town this is – everything you could want – church, chapel, cinemas, a Rugby team, Woolworth's."

The girls cheered.

"We're going to Old Road School. Everyone's there, getting ready for you. Bit of a rugby scrum. Lovely," he said.

It was a gray little town. The streets looked narrow and old-fashioned after busy London. You could smell the soot and something else, sharp and unpleasant. "Tinworks," the bus driver told them.

When they got to the school, they filed into the gymnasium, where tables and chairs had been set up, and they were offered tea and biscuits.

"We are most pleased to welcome you to Wales, and we hope your stay is a pleasant one," said a gentleman, who spoke almost as if he were singing, his voice gentle and melodious.

At that moment the doors opened and a stream of people came in and surged round the girls, looking them over, reading the names on the labels, and often talking to each other in a strange language.

"Must be Welsh," said Lucy, who'd been in the same compartment as Marianne.

Miss Lacey said something to the gentleman and he announced, "Please tell one of the teachers or helpers which child you are taking and give an address. Can't have anyone getting lost, can we now?" Hardly anyone paid attention to him. The youngest and prettiest girls were quickly signed out. The man spoke in Welsh to the people.

"Oh, David, look – twins. There's alike they are."

"And how old are you, dear? Twelve – well now, that's good. Nice and tidy, are you?"

A lady asked Marianne, "What's your name?"

"I'm Marianne Kohn."

Miss Barry was quickly at Marianne's side. "Mary Anne is a Jewish refugee from Germany."

The lady took a step back. "Oh, I see. No thanks, then. Jewish and German? I don't think so. Wouldn't be proper, would it?" she said to Miss Barry, as if turning down some strange exotic fruit. She moved on.

Slowly the hall emptied. At last only Lucy, two older girls who Marianne didn't know, and Marianne were left.

"I know what's wrong with me," said Marianne, "but why haven't *you* been chosen?"

Before they could answer, Miss Barry said, "There's absolutely nothing wrong with any of you. The billeting officer, Mr. Evans, hadn't expected quite so many of us. Now he's made arrangements for you for the next couple of nights, till more permanent billets can be found. Doreen and Jeannie, you're going to sleep in the nurses' hostel. Some of the probationers are only a little older than you are. Lucy and Mary Anne, you go to a Methodist home for girls. Get a good night's sleep, and don't worry."

"Excuse me, Miss Barry," said Lucy, "I've broken my glasses. I sat on them on the bus and cracked the lenses. I can't see properly."

"We'll sort everything out tomorrow," said Miss Barry. "Doreen and Jeannie, come with me. Goodnight, girls." She left Marianne and Lucy with a distracted billeting officer.

The girls picked up their luggage.

"Follow me, then. We don't have far to go," said Mr. Evans.

· 18 ·

"A poor start"

It was almost dark. A few dim streetlights came on. It began to drizzle. They walked up a hill, lined on both sides with small terraced houses. The houses were a uniform gray, the front windows hung with muslin curtains and the front steps level with the cobbled pavement.

Mr. Evans hurried them past a pub – the smell of beer, the sounds of laughter and foreign words spilled over onto the street. A group of men came out, beer mugs in hand, their mufflers shining white under the lamps. They were singing. One of them raised his hand in greeting to Mr. Evans.

"Friday night, see?" said Mr. Evans, as if to apologize to the small visitors for this sign of life. "Members of the Rugby team, the Scarlets, always meet here on Friday nights. Famous we are for Rugby. Beat the Australian Wallabies in 1908. I grew up going to the games in Stradey Park. My father was on the team there.

He's passed away now." He hummed sadly, then he said, "'*Sospan Fach* – Little Saucepan.' I marched to it in the last war. '*Sospan fach yn berwiar y tân,*'" he sang softly.

"What does it mean?" asked Lucy.

"It sounds like 'saucepan,'" said Marianne.

"Quite right, *bach*. Clever girl, you are. It's the theme song of the Scarlets. A silly little ditty about a small saucepan on the stove, and a little cat who knocks it over. But there's nothing silly about our team. Rugby gives us our pride. Wars come and go; the mines shut down; nothing stops us so long as our little red saucepans are on top of the goalposts. Not far now. Getting tired, are you?"

The men's voices grew fainter. "*Dai bach y sowidiwr, Dai bach y sowidiwr . . .*"

Mr. Evans sang along, translating for them: "Young Dai, a soldier, young Dai, a soldier."

They walked along streets that all looked alike. Everywhere the coal tips looked down on them. As they passed a big square building, there came the most beautiful singing Marianne had ever heard. She paused for a moment to listen.

"I can see you like music. That's a good sign, *bach*. Chapel, are you?" Mr. Evans didn't wait for a reply. "Ebenezer Chapel, built in 1891. Fine choir. Well, come along; it's getting late."

They stopped, at last, in front of a row house at the end of a side street. A woman in a shapeless black dress answered the door.

"Ah, Matron, *shwmae heno* – how are you tonight? Here are the two evacuees. Very good of you, I'm sure, to find room for them. This is Lucy and this is Mary Anne."

"Come in, Mr. Evans. Don't stand on the step. A cup of tea before you go?"

"If it's no trouble, Matron."

"I'll just show the girls upstairs." Matron led them up a narrow stairway. "Lucy, you can go in this room, and Mary Anne in here. Unpack, and then come downstairs." She hurried back to Mr. Evans.

Lucy whispered, "I wish we were in the same room. Should we knock?"

Marianne said, "I think so. I'll see you in about ten minutes and we'll go down together."

The rooms were next to each other, the paint peeling off the doors. The girls looked at each other and knocked. They walked in.

Marianne said, "Hello, I'm Marianne Kohn. I'm an evacuee from London."

Two girls sat on the narrow beds farthest from the door. There was a chair beside each bed. The unoccupied bed, made up with a gray blanket, was set against the damp-looking wall. The girls got on with their knitting.

"How far are you gone?" said one to Marianne, not looking up.

"I beg your pardon? I don't understand what you mean," she replied.

"Well, if you don't want to tell us, that's your business, isn't it?"

Marianne put her suitcase on the bed and unlocked it.

"Matron will kill you if you put that on the bed," said the other girl, who was dressed in a loose blue smock. "On the floor – use some common sense, can't you?"

Marianne moved her case, and said, "Please, where is the lavatory?"

The first girl put down her knitting and stood up and walked towards Marianne. Her waist was huge and Marianne realized that she was expecting a baby. Both girls looked a couple of years older than Marianne.

"The lavatory, my dear? Well, now, we don't have those fancy London ways here. The running water comes from the sky." She went to a small window and pointed. "*Tŷ bach* – the lavatory to you – is out there, and in my condition, don't expect me to walk down and show you," the girl said.

Marianne replied, "I'm sorry, we just came off the train. I don't even know where we are."

The girls started to laugh. One of them said, "You're in the Methodist Home for Unmarried Mothers. A disgrace to the community, we are. By the looks of you, you've come to the wrong place."

Marianne didn't know what to say. The girls turned to each other and began to speak quickly in Welsh, staring at her and laughing.

Marianne opened the door and fled downstairs.

"Mary Anne, wait for me." Lucy was behind her. "I can't imagine what Miss Barry would say if she knew we were *here*."

Marianne said, "They're not exactly friendly, are they? It's not for long – only a day or two she said."

Matron appeared at the bottom of the stairs. "There you are. Mr. Evans had to leave. What a busy man he is, and all this extra work." She looked at them accusingly. "Come in the kitchen." She put a bowl of bread and milk in front of each of the girls and waited. Marianne picked up her spoon.

"Before grace?" Matron spoke in a shocked whisper.

Lucy looked at Marianne through her cracked lenses and said, "I'll do it. For what we are about to receive, may the Lord make us truly thankful."

Marianne joined in the amen.

Matron said, "When you've finished, wash your bowls in the scullery. Be quick now, it's late."

When they'd eaten, the girls carried their bowls into a narrow flagstone scullery, and rinsed the dishes in a bowl of water that stood in the sink. The water was cold. There was a greasy towel hanging on a nail by the door, and they used that to dry the dishes.

"The privy is at the end of the path," said Matron. She took a key from the pocket of her dress and unlocked the back door. The yard was dark and smelt of cats.

"Wait for me, Mary Anne. I'm terrified of spiders and I can't see properly," said Lucy.

When they came back to the house, Matron told them to wash at the pump by the back door and handed them a sliver of soap and the same greasy towel they'd used to dry the dishes. As soon as they were back inside, she locked the scullery door behind them.

"Breakfast at seven, and make your beds before you come down." She watched them go up, and then went back into the kitchen.

"Goodnight, Lucy," said Marianne. "Sleep well."

"If Miss Barry doesn't come and get us tomorrow, I'm going to catch the first train back home," said Lucy, and went into her room.

Marianne thought she heard sounds of scuffling behind the door. When she opened it, she saw that one of the girls was hunched over her open suitcase. "What are you doing with my things?" asked Marianne, horrified.

"Did you hear that, Margaret? Did you hear her accuse me? Are you calling me a thief?" The girl got clumsily to her feet.

"You were going through my case," said Marianne.

"You're a dirty spy." The girl held an envelope in her hand.

Marianne tried to stay calm. She said, "Please give me that letter. It's from my mother in Germany."

"Dilys, you were right. She *is* a spy," said Margaret, and got out of bed to stand by her friend.

"I'm too young to be a spy. I'm only twelve years old. My mother sent me here to be safe from the Nazis. I'm Jewish," said Marianne.

Margaret crossed herself, and Dilys gave a scream of horror. "Christ killer," Dilys said. "You did that." And she pushed

Marianne forward and forced her to look at the picture on the wall that showed Christ hanging on the cross. Marianne stared at the nails driven through His feet and hands, and the gashes in His side.

The door opened and Matron stood in the doorway. The girls scuttled back to their beds.

"What is the meaning of this? What is going on here?"

Dilys replied, "She's a Jew."

Margaret added, "She gets letters from Germany. She's a spy."

Marianne burst out, "They have no right to touch my things. They went through my suitcase. I want my letter back." And she went up to Dilys and snatched the envelope out of her hand.

"Oh, my poor baby, a Jew," wailed Dilys and put her hands protectively over her stomach. "He'll be marked."

"Come with me. Bring your things," said Matron, "and not one more word. Be quick, now." She pushed Marianne out of the door. "Go down," she said.

They went downstairs.

"You'll wait here till I come back. Don't move."

Matron took the shawl that was hanging on the hook, put it over her head, and opened the front door. Marianne heard her lock the door from the outside. She was too angry to be frightened. After a while, she sat on the bottom stair, her hands over her ears to shut out the words "Christ killer," which Dilys and Margaret called from the upstairs landing.

After a long time, Matron returned. Mr. Evans was with her. He picked up Marianne's suitcase without a word. The door slammed behind them.

"Now then, *bach*," he said, "that was a poor start." They walked in silence for a long time, then they stopped in front of a small row house. It was very dark. Mr. Evans rapped on the door.

· 19 ·

The Witch

A very old lady, wearing a lace cap over her wispy gray hair and a shawl over her nightgown, opened the door. She was stooped over, and was only a little taller than Marianne.

"*Y ferch, Mam*," said Mr. Evans.

He turned to Marianne and said, "My mother has very little English. I told her, 'Here's the little girl.' You sleep well now. This is just for one night; I'll find you a billet tomorrow. *Nos da, Mam*. Goodnight, Mary Anne." Mr. Evans disappeared into the dark street.

Mrs. Evans beckoned Marianne inside and made signs to her to follow up the stairs. Mrs. Evans' progress was slow. She hung on to the bannisters, wheezing at every step, threatening to extinguish the candle she held in her other hand. Once upstairs, she maneuvered herself onto the double bed, which took up most of the space in the airless small room.

All Marianne could think of was witches – every witch in every story she'd ever read. She looked at the "witch's" teeth floating in the glass on the narrow mantel. *Do I really have to sleep with this toothless old woman?*

There was a porcelain chamber pot at the foot of the bed. Marianne shivered, though the room was hot and stuffy.

The "witch" made signs for Marianne to get in bed beside her. She kept repeating "*Dech y gwely,*" and patting the pillow beside her. "Come to bed."

Marianne stood at the door, wondering if she dare flee.

After a long time, Mrs. Evans, sounding each word with great difficulty, said again, "Come to bed." She patted the space that was waiting for Marianne, and smiled a very unlike witch's smile, showing clean pink gums. *How hard this poor lady is trying to make herself understood. She's been woken in the middle of the night, and now she is willing to share her bed with me.*

"Thank you," said Marianne. She took a step into the room, undid her suitcase, and pulled out her nightdress. The old lady smiled and nodded at her, blew out the candle, then turned on her side away from Marianne.

Marianne climbed into bed, and lay near the very edge.

"*Nos da* – Goodnight," said Mrs. Evans. They slept.

When Marianne woke up the next morning, the old lady – and the teeth in the glass – were gone. She went downstairs and straight into the kitchen.

"*Bore da* – Good morning," said Mrs. Evans, and pointed Marianne into the tiny scullery. She opened the back door, and

Marianne walked along the path set with flagstones to the lavatory. Someone, perhaps Mr. Evans, had whitewashed the walls. There wasn't a spider in sight.

When she got back, Mrs. Evans was pouring hot water from the kettle into a tin bowl. She put out a clean towel and a piece of soap for Marianne to wash.

When Marianne had finished, she went into the kitchen and Mrs. Evans handed her a plate of brown bread and butter. "*Bara menyn*," she said, pointing to the food.

Marianne repeated the words. *Welsh is quite easy!* Mrs. Evans seemed very pleased. She poured Marianne a cup of tea, and then sat in her rocking chair by the big oven and watched her eat her breakfast. Although the kitchen was small, it was very cosy. As well as the big black oven, there was a tall cupboard full of brightly colored plates and cups. A crocheted rug lay in front of the brass fender. On the mantelpiece were two china figurines and a doll wearing a black hat, red flannel dress, and white apron.

A cat purred under the table. If she had noticed Mrs. Evans' black cat last night, she would truly have been convinced she was in the house of a witch.

Marianne said, "Your house is beautiful."

Mrs. Evans nodded and smiled. "*Diolch* – Thanks," she said. Her teeth moved when she spoke.

There was a knock on the door and Mr. Evans came in. "*Bore da, Mam.* Good morning, Mary Anne. Had a good sleep, did you?" He did not wait for an answer, but started an animated conversation in Welsh with his mother, who nodded and interrupted softly from time to time. Then they'd both stop talking, look at Marianne pityingly, shake their heads, and continue.

At last Mr. Evans sat down and said to Marianne, "Well now, *bach*."

"Please, what does *bach* mean? I thought it was the name of a composer."

Mr. Evans laughed. "I knew last night you were musical, young lady. It's the choir you'll have to be joining. No, no, *bach* just means 'little,' or 'dear.' Now, I'm pleased to say, I have found a very nice home for you, with Mr. and Mrs. Roberts. They are happy to give a home to a little girl. So get your things and we'll be on our way."

When Marianne came down with her suitcase, she said, "Please, will you tell your mother 'thank you very much'? She is so kind."

Mr. Evans said, "Tell her *diolch*."

Marianne went up to Mrs. Evans, said *diolch*, and curtsied. Mrs. Evans pushed herself up from her chair and patted Marianne's cheek with her gnarled fingers.

When they got outside and were walking down the hill, Mr. Evans said, "You must be a very good girl for Mrs. Roberts. A sad time she's had, and her such a pillar of the chapel. Never misses a meeting."

Marianne's stomach gave a warning lurch. "Is this a temporary billet?" she asked.

"Oh no, indeed. Mrs. Roberts is looking forward to having a child in the house again. You'll be settling down there now."

· 20 ·

A Good Home

The white lace curtains of 66 Queen Victoria Road moved slightly. Marianne straightened her shoulders. The front door opened.

"*Bore da*, Mr. Evans. Come in quick, do. Don't stand outside."

They walked in.

"This is the little girl, Mary Anne Kohn, we were talking about," Mr. Evans said.

Marianne could guess the kinds of things they'd been saying, but he was a very nice man and was doing his best for her. There was no reason to feel so apprehensive. *Why do I feel so uneasy?* she wondered, her stomach lurching again.

"There's skinny, she is. Soon fatten you up, we will. *Diolch*, Mr. Evans, for bringing her. There's a shame you working Saturday. Lots to do with all these 'vacuees, I dare say, and war not started yet. Sometimes I think it's a blessing my Elisabeth isn't here to see it. Very sensitive she was, as you know, Mr. Evans."

Marianne wondered who Elisabeth was. This lady seemed to have a lot to say; perhaps she was lonely. Was there a Mr. Roberts?

"And how's your dear mother, Mr. Evans?"

"*Mam's* as well as can be expected. Eighty years old last month. Took a great fancy to your little Mary Anne here."

Your? She hadn't been in the house two minutes; she wasn't a parcel to be handed over.

"Well, better be off, Mrs. Roberts. More billets to find. Good-bye, Mary Anne."

"Thank you very much, Mr. Evans. *Diolch*," Marianne said.

"Proper little Welsh girl you're getting to be. Good-bye, both."

Mr. Evans hurried away and Marianne and her new foster mother were alone.

"You can call me Auntie Vi, short for Violet. Later on, I expect you'll be calling me *Mam*," said Mrs. Roberts.

Marianne already knew that *mam* was Welsh for mother. *Hasn't Mr. Evans told Mrs. Roberts I already have a mother?*

Auntie Vi was small and slim. Her hair was done up in heavy metal curlers, which poked through the scarf round her head. She was very tidy in a dark blue dress and little flowered pinafore. The house smelt of polish.

"Come along, and I'll show you everything. This is the front room – we use it only for special occasions." She straightened the lace curtains in the tiny window. It was a square little room, with a small sofa and two matching armchairs. There was a narrow side table, with a vase of dried flowers on it and a leather-bound bible. The floor shone. "We had the funeral tea for Elisabeth here. Lovely, it was. That's her picture on the mantelpiece."

A serious-looking child stared down at Marianne from a gilt-framed photograph. She looked like her mother.

"Taken just before she died. There were so many at the tea for her, we had to sit down in shifts. Ten years old, she was." She touched Marianne's hair. "I'd brush her hair every night a hundred times – so silky. Kept all her things. I'll show you."

They went upstairs to a bedroom that was like a shrine to the dead child.

Marianne said, "I'm twelve, not ten."

"Well, never mind. A pity, but never mind." Mrs. Roberts sighed deeply. "Look, there's a picture of Elisabeth when she was four. Like Shirley Temple, she looked. I've kept a lock of her hair."

Marianne hoped Mrs. Roberts wouldn't show it to her.

"Remind me, *bach*, to show it to you. It's in a locket – I wear it on Sundays. . . ." She pulled open a drawer. "Her clothes are still folded just the way they always were. You won't touch the doll, will you?"

Marianne looked at the wax doll sitting on the center of the chest of drawers. The doll's eyes were fixed, so that they remained wide open.

"Ordered it from Cardiff, I did. Elisabeth was lying in that bed, gasping for breath, and we put the doll in her arms. When she died her dadda wanted to bury it with her, but I said no. I look at it when I dust her room. Every day I dust and think about her. You can dust and keep it nice, can't you, Mary Anne? Dust your little sister's room?" Her singsong voice was like a chant.

Marianne nodded, too mesmerized to speak.

Mrs. Roberts said, "You can hang your clothes in the wardrobe. I've pushed Elisabeth's dresses to one side. And the bottom drawer of the chest is empty. Perfect for two little sisters sharing. Get unpacked now, and then come downstairs."

"Thank you, Auntie Vi."

Marianne tried the window. Thank goodness it opened. It had stopped raining. The coal tips looked black and clear, framing the horizon, walling her in.

She put her things away, and then put her nightdress into the bed. Something soft touched her hand – Marianne screamed.

Mrs. Roberts must have been waiting outside. She rushed in. "What is it? Have you a pain?" She placed her hand on Marianne's forehead.

"I'm fine. I was surprised, that's all. I felt something touch my hand when I put my nightdress under the sheet."

Mrs. Roberts pulled a white satin case from the bedclothes.

"Beautiful, isn't it? See how I've embroidered her name on the cover. Now, if you're very careful, you can keep your nightdress in it too."

Marianne began to perspire. She felt dizzy. The room was very stuffy. "Oh no, thank you. I don't want to spoil it."

"Plenty of room for you both." Her voice was firm. She closed the window. "Don't want you getting chilled. Come on down now. Mr. Roberts will be in for his dinner at one. Saturday's a split shift. Lucky he is working for the railway. All through the Depression, he was in work. Shorter hours, of course, but always something coming in. Not like the colliers – hard times they had. Still, things are bound to pick up now that we're going to war. There's always a silver lining, isn't there? Now you've time to go out to play for a bit." She handed Marianne a ball. "Here's Elisabeth's ball."

Auntie Vi talked nonstop. Her voice was very soft, and her sentences went up at the end as though she were asking a question, but Marianne could tell she was used to having things the way she wanted.

"Thank you, Auntie Vi. May I go for a walk? Not far. I'll leave the ball with you so I won't lose it."

"Don't be long, then. I don't want you catching cold."

"But it's summer," said Marianne."

"Wear your blazer." Auntie Vi's voice was gently insistent.

Marianne didn't argue. "Good-bye, Auntie Vi."

Larver Bread

Marianne walked down the road, wondering if she was imagining things. There seemed to be something awfully strange about this new "aunt." Now she understood what Mr. Evans had meant when he said, "A sad time she's had." *It must be dreadful to lose an only child. No wonder Auntie Vi seems peculiar.* Marianne wondered what it would be like to sleep in a bed in which someone had died. A good thing she didn't believe in ghosts.

If Bridget were here, she'd say, "Hope she changed the sheets." She had so much to tell Bridget, and it was only four days since they'd said good-bye.

Marianne crossed the street at the end of Victoria Road and was careful to make a note of the buildings, so that she wouldn't lose her way. Not like her first day in England! On the left was a big gray chapel called Zion, and across the street was the library. She went up the steps and through the glass doors. A lady behind the counter smiled at her.

"You must be one of the London evacuees. Ever so many came in today. There's smart you all look in your blazers."

She handed Marianne a form and said, "Get your auntie to sign and then you can take out a book."

"Thank you," said Marianne.

She was just about to cross the street to go back for dinner, when she heard her name.

"Mary Anne. Wait." It was Lucy. "Oh, Mary Anne, I'm so glad to see you. I'm sorry about last night. How are you? I should have come out and helped you. I was afraid to get into trouble too. Sorry," she said again.

"It doesn't matter. Are you still at that awful place?" asked Marianne.

"No. One of the teachers came and got me quite early. I don't think they knew what was going on yesterday. What a muddle. Can't wait for school to start so we can find out about everyone."

"Me, too," said Marianne. "Wonder how Hilary's getting on in her billet?"

"Can you imagine her face if the lavatory's a wooden hut full of spiders?" said Lucy.

They laughed.

"What's your billet like?" Marianne asked.

"Crowded. It's a little house. I share the back bedroom with the boys – three-year-old twins. Mrs. Taylor's father lives there, too. He sleeps in the kitchen so he can keep warm. Only speaks Welsh, I think. Uncle Tom's down the mines; haven't seen him yet. When I got there, Auntie Ethel said, 'There's sensible you look. Thank goodness they sent me a girl. I'm all behind this morning. Come in, *bach*.' We had a cup of tea and Welsh cakes. I haven't even unpacked yet. She said, 'I hope you're a good sleeper. Gareth was up all night with toothache, and Peter cries to keep him company.' Then she asked me if I'd mind picking up something at the market. Do you want to come with me? It's not far – I asked at the library."

Marianne said, "I used to like markets once." They walked towards the market hall. "Will you be alright in your billet?"

Lucy replied, "I'm good at getting things done. You know, organizing, and she seemed glad to have me there, not just because she's going to get money for my keep. What about your place?"

Marianne said cautiously, "Auntie Vi seems very nice, a bit strange, but that's because her little girl died. School will start soon, so I won't be there that much, will I?"

Lucy said, "We'll be home before Christmas, I bet. Even if there is a war, it won't last any time."

Marianne wondered where she'd go. She supposed she'd have to go back to Aunt Vera's, if she'd have her.

The heat and smells and noise of the market washed over them like a wave. There were stalls outside on the cobbles, and more inside the big hall. They went in past bake counters piled high with floury buns, Welsh cakes, pies, and tarts oozing with jam and fruit. Vegetables on carts looked as if they'd been picked moments before – drops of rain shone on the wavy cabbage leaves and bits of rich black soil clung to the carrots and sprouts. A butcher in a blood-spattered white apron was arranging feathered chickens in a row. Rabbits hung from metal hooks, their eyes glazed, their necks broken, their fur matted where a drop of blood had trickled down.

Marianne looked away. Lucy asked the woman at the cheese stall if she could tell them where Mrs. Jones had her stall. The beaming huge woman looked at them and laughed. "From London, are you?" She cut them each a corner of crumbly white cheese and said, "Welsh cheese from Carmathen. You won't get that in London."

"*Diolch*," the girls said, and the woman smiled at them even more broadly.

"Jones. Now there's Jones the Fish and Jones Shoes and Jones China – which is it you want, *bach*? A popular name in these parts." She laughed again.

Lucy spelled out the words on her paper: BARA LAWR – LARVER BREAD.

The woman said, "Mrs. Jones is straight down this aisle and then turn left at Sammy's – SAMUEL & SON, TAILOR. Can't miss it, they're right beside each other." She turned to her next customer.

The tailor had bolts of colored fabrics and rows of shirts and dresses on wire hangers, hung on a wooden pole. Sammy was a little old man in a black waistcoat and short leather apron. His chin was stubbly, and he spoke in an accent that wasn't like the Welsh around them. Marianne heard him say, "Only for you, Mrs. Davis, I make a special price, and I throw in a little remnant. *Nu* – Well, what do you say?" He held a length of dark blue material.

"Mary Anne, come *on*. Here it is." The sign said JONES — BARA LAWR — LARVER BREAD. Lucy was looking at strands of dark green lengths of some kind of vegetable. "This is what I'm supposed to buy. What is it?"

Marianne said, "It looks like spinach."

The woman said, "Try a piece; tell me how you like it."

Marianne said, "It tastes of fish, a bit like chopped herring."

"Seaweed," said Mrs. Jones. "Very healthy it is too. A pound, is it, you want?" She wrapped the larver bread in newspaper, and Lucy paid her.

"That's the most disgusting thing I've ever tasted," said Lucy. "I don't know how you could say you like it. Come on, let's buy something to take the taste away. There's MYFANWY'S SWEETS over there."

Marianne turned round and saw Sammy the tailor looking after them curiously. He reminded her of the peddlers who'd sometimes come to her grandmother's back door years ago.

"You choose, Mary Anne, and I'll treat, to make up for last night."

There were jars of liquorice wound in coils like snakes, mints, red and yellow pear drops, small white triangular packets of sherbet, black-and-white bull's-eyes, humbugs guaranteed to change color, slabs of chocolate, and brightly wrapped toffees all in tall glass jars.

The big market clock began to strike 12:30. Marianne pointed to the striped aniseed balls, twelve for a penny. Lucy divided them equally.

"Thanks awfully," said Marianne, her cheek bulging. "We'd better go. Don't want to be late on my first day."

"Thanks for coming with me. See you in school. 'Bye. Oh, I forgot to tell you, my foster parents keep a pig in the coal shed." Lucy waved, and they ran back to their billets.

Marianne found her way easily. She saw Mrs. Roberts looking down the road for her.

"There you are, *bach*. Afraid you'd got lost. Come in now and meet your Uncle Dai. Longing to meet his new little girl, he is."

· 22 ·

A New Name

Marianne wiped her feet on the little strip of carpet inside the front door. It seemed odd to walk in straight from the street, just over the step and inside. Uncle Dai was sitting at the kitchen table eating soup.

"Here she is," said Auntie Vi proudly. "Sent in answer to our prayers."

Uncle Dai put down his spoon, wiped his hands on his trousers, and said, "Well, well. Let me have a look at you. Come and shake hands. I'm pleased to meet you." Auntie Vi beamed.

Marianne said, "How do you do, Sir?"

"Uncle Dai, Mairi."

"Please, Uncle Dai, my name is Marianne."

"Mary, Mary Anne. Mair in Welsh. A pretty Welsh name for a nice little girl living in a Welsh home. Mairi it is, then. Right, *Mam*?"

"Whatever you say, Dai."

But Marianne had the idea that Auntie Vi had suggested it.

"Mairi it shall be. Mairi Roberts. Got a ring to it."

Marianne wondered if all the other girls in her class were being renamed.

"Sit down, Mairi, and eat your soup. Elisabeth loved my lamb broth. Those last days we had her, it was all she could get down. Do you like it, Mairi?"

"It's very good, thank you." Marianne was beginning to dread every mention of poor little Elisabeth.

"Uncle Dai said, "Church or chapel, Mairi?"

"In London I went to church, but at home in –"

Uncle Dai interrupted her. "Chapel it is. Baptists we are. Wait till you hear the sermon tomorrow. Reverend Thomas guiding us down the paths of righteousness. Your auntie goes to meetings twice a week and sings in the chapel choir; beautiful voice she has."

Marianne offered to do the dishes.

"No, no, you go and play in the garden. I'll just heat up the kettle. Take the ball now," said Auntie Vi, and handed it to her.

Marianne went out into the back. The yard was narrow, with dusty-looking grass. The coal shed took up most of the space. She saw Mrs. Roberts peering at her through the scullery window.

Marianne began to bounce the ball, obediently, doing the accompanying actions.

Charlie Chaplin went to France
To teach the ladies how to dance
And this is what he taught them
Heel toe
Over we go
Don't forget to twist.

Marianne wondered what Elisabeth had died of. Perhaps from breathing in the fine dust that had already turned her white blouse gray.

She didn't feel like playing ball anymore. She was twelve, not a little girl. She leaned against the coal shed, shutting her eyes against the glare of the sun. In London she'd never thought about where coal came from. It was just there, brought in from outside in the brass coal scuttle. Warming cold rooms. Coal so shiny black it sparkled. What must it be like working day after day in all that blackness? Like moles burrowing underground. *Are the miners ever afraid? Don't they miss seeing the sun?*

Marianne went back into the kitchen.

"Excuse me, Auntie Vi, the lady at the library said if you sign this form, I can join the library."

"Library, is it? Dai, you sign it, please, before you go back to work."

"Give me the card. Clever as well as pretty, are you?" He signed it.

They are so nice to me. I couldn't wish for a better billet, so why do I feel so uncomfortable?

When she reached the library, Marianne sat down on the wooden bench in the cool lobby and tried to think things out. How could she explain to anyone that she felt as if she couldn't breathe, that these kind people were smothering her? No one could be part of a family that quickly. She knew Mr. and Mrs. Roberts were looking for someone to fill the gap left by Elisabeth, but they weren't giving her time. How could they love someone they'd only known for five minutes? It was like being sucked down into a whirlpool – no way to escape. It sounded silly to be frightened of people being nice. She looked at the clock. *How many hours till bedtime? Tonight I'll have to go to sleep with that awful doll staring at me. Perhaps I can move it to the floor and put it back in the morning before Auntie Vi notices.*

Marianne handed in her form. She asked the librarian if there were any stories about Wales, and was given a book of Welsh legends. The librarian told her about Merlin the magician, who had been born in South Wales and became advisor to King Arthur and his knights. "He will come and save the land if we need him," the librarian said seriously. "Only sleeping he is, in a cave in the mountains."

That night it took Marianne a long time to go to sleep. She heard Uncle Dai come upstairs and go to bed.

Something woke her. She felt cold lips on her forehead, and then a whispered "*Nos da*, Elisabeth."

She lay very still and, from under almost closed lids, watched Auntie Vi go to the chest and put the doll back in its usual spot. Then she shut the window and went out.

Marianne waited five minutes, then crept out of bed and opened the window again. There was a moon. *I know you're out there somewhere, Mutti. Please come soon – please come and get me.* Then she took the doll and put her facedown on the chest, and went to sleep holding her bear.

· 23 ·

"It is war"

After breakfast on Sunday, Auntie Vi tied Marianne's hair with a ribbon she took from Elisabeth's drawer, and they set off for Greenfield Chapel. There was a big sign outside, which said: GREATER LOVE HATH NO MAN THAN HE LAY DOWN HIS LIFE FOR HIS FRIENDS. The roof was almost flat, not like a church spire. But as the sermon was mostly in Welsh, Marianne couldn't tell whether there were any other differences. It was very noisy.

The reverend shouted up to the rafters and to the congregation. *No chance of anyone dozing off here!* The only good part was the singing. Marianne didn't think their school choir could ever produce music that was so magical.

The voices stopped suddenly when the sound of the air-raid siren signaling danger filled the air with a great wailing, floating up and down in a terrifying series of notes.

A man hurried up the aisle and whispered something in the preacher's ear.

"It is war," Reverend Thomas said in English. "God will punish the wicked and bless the meek. Let us pray now for a conclusion to the evil that fills the world."

The prayers in Welsh went on until the long, one-note sound of the all clear.

Their walk home through the streets was slow. Every few minutes they stopped to talk to neighbors, whose comments in both languages ranged from how the Germans would never conquer the French, to the atrocities in Belgium in the last war, and to the dire forecasts of parachutists landing on the beach momentarily.

Marianne stuffed Elisabeth's hair ribbon in her pocket. War meant only one thing to her at this moment – she and her parents were on opposite sides of the English Channel. There would be no more letters. She was alone.

Lucy had said they'd be back in London by Christmas. Would the war be over by then? But what if Lucy was wrong? How many more birthdays and holidays would there be, spent apart from her father and mother?

After dinner, when she had helped Auntie Vi clear up, Marianne excused herself and went to write to Bridget. She'd just written the date – September 3, 1939 – when Auntie Vi called her downstairs. "Mairi, come down here, please."

Marianne did as she was told, though she felt like saying, "Please call me by my real name." Her name was all she had left of her life with her parents. Changing her name couldn't turn her into Auntie Vi's daughter.

"Look who's here to say hello, *bach*. It's Mrs. Jenkins from next door. Come and say *shwmae*."

"*Shwmae*, Mair. Now you call me Auntie Blodwen," said their neighbor.

"*Shwmae*, Auntie Blodwen," said Marianne. *Another aunt!* Then she said to Auntie Vi, "I was just going to write a letter to my friend Bridget in Canada."

The two women looked at each other. "No, Mairi. Not on a Sunday. Sinful, that is."

Mrs. Jenkins said, "Terrible to declare war on a Sunday. They should have waited."

"There's glad I am our Elisabeth was spared this day," said Auntie Vi. "I'll just go and make a pot of tea, Blodwen."

"And where are you from, Mair, *bach*? You don't sound like a girl from London. Not that I have much to do with people from there. Swansea's as far as I go. Cardiff once or twice to see my *mam*."

"I've been living in London since last year," said Marianne. "But before that I lived in Germany." The moment she saw Auntie Blodwen's face, she realized her mistake.

"Never! So you speak German, then? Did you ever see Hitler?"

"I don't speak German anymore, and Jews kept away from Hitler."

Auntie Vi came in and poured tea. Mrs. Jenkins drank hers so quickly, it was a wonder her tongue wasn't scalded.

"Have a Welsh cake, Blodwen, do," said Auntie Vi.

"No, no, I must be getting back. Company's coming for supper." She was suddenly in a great hurry.

145

Perhaps I shouldn't have said anything about coming from Germany. People might not understand that I'm a refugee, that I'm more anti-Hitler than any of them. Or is it because I said I'm Jewish?

Marianne went upstairs to get her book, then remembered she wasn't supposed to do that on Sunday. "Can I go for a walk, Auntie Vi?"

"Don't forget to take your gas mask, and be home in twenty minutes."

As Marianne walked down the street, she saw Mrs. Jenkins on the step of her house. She went inside quickly and shut the door.

Is it all going to start again? Even here?

That night Uncle Dai climbed up and down the stepladder to make sure all the blackout curtains were in place.

Auntie Vi came in with her Sunday face on.

"Don't tell me it's Sunday," said Uncle Dai. "If the German planes bomb the street because they can see our light, that'll be a bigger sin, especially as I've signed on as a warden for A.R.P. duty. Mairi, *bach*, hold the ladder steady, please."

Now seemed a good time to say it. "Excuse me, Uncle Dai," Marianne said. "Would you mind calling me by my real name?"

She'd been wanting to ask him ever since she got here. She had to keep some of her old self. She'd start with her name.

"Now, we don't want to be putting on airs like those stuck-up Londoners, Mairi, *bach*."

"Well, Uncle Dai, I'm not really a Londoner, and . . ." Marianne faltered.

What could she say? She didn't really know who she was anymore.

Uncle Dai got off the stepladder. "Your parents sent you away. We are taking care of you, right?"

Auntie Vi came in. She *must* have been listening.

"Leave my little girl alone, Dai. It's the Lord's will. They took my Elisabeth and sent me Mairi. Her parents sent her away for a purpose. Stands to reason. We'll do what's right and proper. You'll start Sunday school next week."

· 24 ·

"Dirty mochyn"

It was a relief when school started. The students were housed in two separate buildings, in different parts of the town, and were always having to run from one class to the other. Marianne ran to be in time when it was English! She didn't want to miss a word of Jane Austen's *Pride and Prejudice*, which Miss Barry had begun to read with them. She dawdled when it was math. Once she and Celia arrived so late, they had to hide in the cloakroom till recess. It was easy to make excuses and fun until Miss Lacey warned the school, in Assembly one morning, that war or no war, there'd be report cards as usual. Marianne knew that one day her mother would want to see those!

Miss Lacey reminded the girls that they were all one family, that their parents had sent them away to be safe from air-raid attacks, and that they should make the most of their new experiences of living in a Welsh mining town. "Write regularly to your parents and try not to worry them."

Marianne dreaded being told to write to her family. *If only I could!*

When Miss Barry called attendance on the second Monday in their temporary classroom, three girls had gone back to London. Miss Barry said, "Don't keep your problems to yourself. Come and tell me after school, so I can try and help."

That day six girls waited to see her. Marianne had so many worries she didn't know where to start, and she didn't think she could explain things to Miss Barry without sounding emotional, something English girls didn't do! She wrote to Bridget instead, waiting till Auntie Vi was shopping, so she could write without her foster mother peering over her shoulder.

28 September, 1939

Dear Bridget,

I got your letter. Thanks for answering me so quickly. I'm glad you like your aunt and uncle and living in Montreal. It must be awfully hard going to a French school. Are you very behind in the classes? I rather like learning bits of Welsh.

Auntie Vi, who's convinced she's my *mother*, has added another routine to her bedtime visits. Now she says a prayer over me as well as saying *nos da* – the Welsh for 'goodnight.' I think of Lady Macbeth driven mad by grief. Miss Barry says Shakespeare wrote about every human emotion. It's all very well on paper, but I'm afraid to go to sleep at night. Did I tell you Auntie Vi reads tea leaves? She said, "They predicted someone new would be joining the family!"

The school play's going to be *A Midsummer Night's Dream* and I'm Peaseblossom. I've only one word to say: "Ready." Then I have to scratch Bottom's ears. Bottom is the perfect role for Lucy. She's so blind without her spectacles, she bumps into things quite naturally, and is hilarious acting the role of a workman who's been transformed into a donkey. We're performing early in November. Miss Lacey's made a rule that only the sixth formers are allowed out without a grown-up after dark because of the blackout, so rehearsals are mainly during school hours.

The big excitement last week was the visit of the school nurse. Guess who had nits in her hair? Hilary Bartlett Brown. She was in hysterics, you can imagine. We were all sent home with a notice to wash our hair with a special black soap. It reeked. I rinsed my hair in vinegar to take away the smell. Hilary was subdued – for her – for one whole day and then went back to normal.

Mrs. Blodwen Jenkins, next door, heard about the nurse's visit. Nothing's a secret in this town. She said "Dirty *mochyn*" when I passed her door. It means 'dirty pig,' and my hair was clean. You'd think I'd personally brought lice into Wales.

Lucky you, learning to skate. Miss you, Bridget. No, there's no news at all of the family. I wrote to Ruth last week. Hope I get a reply soon – she may know something. Thanks for asking. If ever I hear anything, I'll let you know. It's awful having a German name – people stare at me as if

I'm the enemy. Mrs. Jenkins told everyone in the street where I was born. I hear them whisper about me when I go by and I'm *not* exaggerating.

> Love from Marianne, also known as
> Mary Anne, also known as Mairi.

· 25 ·

"O land of my fathers'"

Auntie Vi said, "Put down the *Echo*, Dai. I want you to listen to Mairi sing the national anthem."

Uncle Dai folded the newspaper, and Marianne sang, and Uncle Dai joined in the *Gwlad, Gwlad* – Wales, Wales part after the first verse.

> *Mae hen wlad fy nhadau yn annwyl imi,*
> *Gwlad beirdd a chantorion, enwogion o fri.*

Marianne knew it almost by heart – she only had to glance at the words occasionally.

"Getting better, you are," said Uncle Dai, "better than the soloist at the Sunday school concert if you go on like this. Elisabeth had a beautiful voice, didn't she, Vi?"

"Beautiful and good through and through she was."

"I'm supposed to find out what the words mean," said Marianne, thankful to change the subject from Elisabeth. "For school."

"Well, now," said Uncle Dai, "glad it is I am that they're taking an interest. It means – are you writing it down, *bach*?"

"Oh yes, Uncle Dai, I am. It's homework."

O land of my fathers'
So precious to me
Proud mother of minstrels
High home of the free.

"And then, *Gwlad*, *Gwlad* means 'Wales, Wales,' my heart is in Wales forever. When I was a boy, my father told me stories of our heroes, how they fought and fell in battle, like they do now."

"Thank you very much," said Marianne. "It's very beautiful. Miss Barry, our teacher, has started a rambling club. 'So that we can learn to appreciate the beauty of the countryside,' she said, and the first meeting is on Saturday morning. So will it be alright if I go after I've cleaned up my room?"

Marianne had planned this speech as carefully as though she were asking for some huge favor, not just a walk. Auntie Vi liked to make all Marianne's plans for her.

"Oh, there's disappointed I am, Mairi," she said. "Uncle Dai's managed to get us a railway pass to Swansea. You know how difficult that is in wartime. I wanted to take you to my sister Lilian.

She hasn't met her new little niece yet." There was a pause, "However, as it's educational, you shall go this time. But I don't want to wait till Christmas to introduce you to your relatives."

"Yes, Auntie Vi, thank you."

Relatives! Auntie Vi is getting worse.

Auntie Vi said, "I won't be that late getting back, long before blackout. Isn't that so, Dai? And you'll come straight home after your walk."

"I will, thank you, Auntie Vi," said Marianne with genuine gratitude. She was having to pretend to be someone she was not, more and more lately. Inside, she was still Marianne, and outside, someone called Mairi.

On Saturday, eight girls from Marianne's class were met by Miss Barry in the town hall square. They walked three miles to Pwll, a small village outside the town, named for the pond around which the small houses clustered. They climbed the hill that overlooked the town beach below.

The beach was strictly out-of-bounds now because of the danger of land mines. It was closed off by barbed wire – not that that had stopped some of the local and London children climbing through and looking for any scrap metal washed in by the tide. Everyone knew that one of the evacuees had gone there with her foster brother on a dare, but no one gave her away.

The girls shared their sandwiches and Marianne swapped her jam ones for Celia's larver bread.

"Doesn't seem fair," Celia said. "You don't have to, Mary Anne."

"I love it. Honestly, I'm not being noble."

"It's true," said Lucy. "She likes it."

Hilary said, "Well, keep away from me. I can't stand that fishy smell."

Miss Barry said, "I brought some Welsh cakes. I made them from my landlady's own recipe. I hope they're good; I've kept them warm in the tin." The cakes disappeared rapidly.

"I never thought about teachers being billeted," said Jane.

"I know," said Miss Barry. "We're not supposed to be human. I miss my little flat in London, and my family and friends the same as you do. My brother is in the R.A.F., so I like to listen to the nine o'clock news, but it's not always convenient to have the wireless on at that time. There's only one room for the family, so then I can't listen. And I miss being able to have a cup of tea whenever I feel like it. Small trivial things, so I do understand how hard it is for you all sometimes."

Suddenly all the girl's grievances poured out, released by Miss Barry's openness with them.

"I dread Sundays, nothing but chapel," said Marjorie.

"At home we have a bathroom. Here I have a bath in the scullery once a week in a tin bath, and I have to use the water after my foster sister, and anyone could walk in and see me," Barbara complained.

"I wish I knew for sure my foster mother doesn't read my letters. I don't have any privacy," Celia said.

"Auntie Dilys complains how much I eat. She says ten and sixpence isn't enough to feed me. We had blood pudding yesterday – I couldn't swallow it, and she said, 'There's gratitude for you,' in a mean voice, trying to make me feel guilty," Rebecca said.

Jane agreed, "That's the worst part, always having to be grateful. She should be grateful to me. I get behind in my homework because she gives me so much to do. All she wants is a maid."

"Nothing's like it is at home. I won't stay here for Christmas. I won't. I want my parents and my own room." Hilary's voice was petulant.

Miss Barry said, "I don't think the war will be over by Christmas. You'll have to be patient like everyone else, Hilary. Perhaps your parents might come down and visit you."

"I like my billet, but I do long for a bit of peace and quiet sometimes. There are so many people in our little house." Lucy smiled as she spoke to soften her words.

"My foster father's afraid they're going to bomb the docks. He thinks Swansea will get it too. What will we do if we're invaded?" asked Anne.

Marjorie said, "My foster father said if the enemy lands, he knows a secret way through the mines. The enemy will never find us."

"Girls, you are perfectly safe. This is why you're here," said Miss Barry.

An airplane flew out of the clouds and low over the village.

"Must be one of ours," said Marianne. "We didn't hear an air-raid warning."

No one said anything, and Hilary looked at her and raised her eyebrows. Marianne knew exactly what she was thinking. If Miss Barry hadn't been there, she would have made some remark to remind Marianne she was from the wrong side, the German side.

Lucy said, "Sugar's going to be rationed any minute, like butter and bacon, my foster mother told me; and my foster father says everyone knows we'll have a really cold winter. He was telling me when he was out of work before the war and on the dole, he and the other colliers had to climb up the coal tips in the dark, secretly, and look for bits of coal to take home."

Miss Barry said, "There was terrible unemployment in the valleys in Wales these last years. Real hardship, and yet the people have taken us in. It can't be easy for them, either. Now it looks like rain and we'd better get back. Next week we'll plan a walk along the old colliery line to the reservoir. Even with the coal tips, it's quite beautiful."

After they'd caught the trolley bus from the terminus in Pwll, and got back to town, Lucy asked Marianne, "Do you want to come and see Horace?"

"Who?" asked Marianne.

"You know, the pig," said Lucy.

"Alright, but I can't stay long."

Lucy lived in a small terraced house near the Rugby grounds. She took Marianne round the back. Marianne could hear someone coughing, gasping for breath.

157

"Who's that? Shouldn't we go and see what's the matter?" Marianne asked Lucy.

"It's Auntie Ethel's father. He's got silicosis. You get it from breathing in coal dust down the mine. He coughs like that all the time. His lungs don't work properly anymore."

She led the way into the small shed that Horace shared with the coal. Horace lay on his side, fierce-looking and enormously fat. It was hard to see very much in the gloom of the shed, but he seemed to be covered with uneven coarse short hair and his skin was a mottled pink and gray.

"He doesn't have much room, does he?" said Marianne.

"It's not like a dog that needs a run in the park. We're fattening him up. He's a nice pig, he eats everything, and he gets all the scraps. We share him with Mr. and Mrs. Bevan next door. He gets out sometimes, when we clean the shed and Mr. Bevan brings clean straw. He's well looked after."

She tickled Horace behind his ears with a stick. Horace curled his lip, showing yellow pointed teeth. "Look at him smiling. I'm quite fond of him. Not too fond, because we'll be eating him for Christmas. Poor old Horace, you'll be bacon and trotters, and roasts and chops and knuckles and ham and ears."

"Ears? Lucy, you're making it up. You're teasing me, aren't you?" Marianne said.

"Why would I?" said Lucy. "Oh, Mary Anne, you are funny. You've seen meat at the butcher's. Horace will be like that. Mrs. Bevan has a wonderful recipe for ears. You clean them, and singe off the hair, and then you boil them till they're soft, and then cut them into strips and fry them with onions."

Marianne rushed out into the yard and closed her eyes. She tried to breathe deeply, so as not to be sick. The air was sooty and smelled of Horace and coal dust and the fumes from the tinworks. The coughing from the kitchen continued. Horace grunted.

Lucy joined her. "Is there anything wrong?" she asked.

"No, it's getting late. I have to be back before blackout. Thanks for showing me Horace. I've never seen a pig that close up before. I never thought about it. At home, you know with my parents, we don't eat pig." Marianne felt such an enormous burden of guilt and homesickness at that moment that tears threatened. She blinked them away.

Lucy said, "I don't mind it here. It's wartime; you get used to it. Horace is my personal war effort. I collect every scrap of food I can find for him. See you Monday."

When Marianne got back, Auntie Vi was making supper. "There's late you are. Mash the potatoes, Mairi. Uncle Dai's going out to play darts. Auntie Lil sent us some pork chops for supper. She said she can't wait to meet her new little niece." She began to fry onions in the pan and added three bright pink pork chops. "Lucky you are, Mairi, always a good meal on the table. Rissoles and chips is what a lot of the 'vacuees live on."

"I'm not very hungry, Auntie Vi. You gave me a lot of sandwiches, thank you."

Auntie Vi's voice hardened. "You're not going to be difficult about your food I hope, Mairi. Be grateful for what the good Lord provides." She placed a chop, potatoes, and cabbage on a plate in front of Marianne.

Uncle Dai said grace. Marianne looked at the tiny bubbles of blood on her meat, where Auntie Vi had speared the chop with a fork. She put a small piece of potato in her mouth. She was afraid it wouldn't go down.

She wanted her mother, her own bed in her own room. At home, whenever she had a stomachache, Mutti would bring her a cup of peppermint tea and a hot water bottle. A tear slid down her cheek onto the cabbage. Instead of missing her mother less lately, she was missing her more and more.

Auntie Vi went to put the kettle on. Marianne began to shiver.

Uncle Dai looked at her. "Got a chill staying out in all weathers. No more rambles for you, *bach*." He slid Marianne's pork chop onto his plate.

Auntie Vi came in from the scullery. "After supper we'll listen to the wireless nice and cosy, while you have a good soak in the tub in front of the fire. Uncle Dai's off any minute."

"Thank you, Auntie Vi. You're very kind to me," said Marianne.

"Only Christian, isn't it? You're our little girl. One happy family."

When Marianne finished her bath, she watched Auntie Vi empty the dregs of her teacup onto a saucer, and peer into the cup.

"Look at the shape of the tea leaves, Mairi – a stranger coming to visit from far away. Off to bed, now." She cleared the teacups absentmindedly.

Later, lying in Elisabeth's bed, Marianne thought of all the people she knew who were far away. All the people she loved best in the world. Of course tea leaves were just superstition, but what if the leaves did mean something?

· 26 ·

"Mam"

One evening a few weeks later, Auntie Vi looked up from the scarf she was knitting for soldiers' Christmas parcels and said, "I want you to call me *Mam*."

Mam? Marianne put down the Latin verbs she was memorizing and stared at Auntie Vi. "But *Mam* means 'Mother,'" Marianne said, shocked.

"Yes. You can be my proper little girl. Like Elisabeth." Mrs. Roberts smiled a blissful smile. Her eyes did not see Marianne at all.

Marianne said, "I have a mother, Auntie Vi. You know that."

"Well, she's not a proper mother, now is she? Sending you to another country. I never heard of a real mother doing that. Not natural, is it? So you'll call me *Mam* if you please, Mairi."

Marianne wanted to scream at her: *She sent me away because she loves me. She's not an unnatural mother. She's not. Stop trying to take her place.* She bit the inside of her cheek hard.

Marianne barely slept that night. After the *"nos da,* Elisabeth" and the bible reading, the ritual of the doll, and the closing of the window followed by Auntie Vi's silent departure, she lay awake for hours, trying to decide what to do.

Next day she was in trouble in school. She'd forgotten to bring her math homework, and there were red crosses against six of the eight problems on Friday's test.

"Mary Anne Kohn," said Miss Joyce in icy tones, "I'm very tired of making allowances for you. You are spoilt and lazy, with disgraceful work habits. There is more to life than dressing up and parading onstage."

The class gasped. Even Hilary didn't smirk.

"You are taking advantage. Your kind always do."

Marianne stood up and said, "Excuse me, Miss Joyce. May I have permission to go home at recess to fetch my homework? And I'm not sure what you mean by 'taking advantage.'"

Every head turned to look at Marianne. Hilary smiled encouragingly at her and Marianne could feel the class shift in their desks, closing ranks around her, almost physically. She might not be one of them exactly, but they were on her side.

"Leave the room and stand in the corridor," thundered Miss Joyce.

Marianne walked out, and closed the door behind her, so softly that it was as much as a statement as if she had slammed it.

Now what? I've really done it. I'll probably be expelled, and then I'll have to stay with Auntie Vi all day. But it did feel good just once to answer back, to stand up and not be silent because she was afraid. Thank goodness the play was over – Miss Joyce might have forbidden her to perform out of spite.

Miss Lacey walked by. "Mary Anne? You are the last student I would have expected to see in the corridor." She entered the classroom and Marianne heard the girls get to their feet and their chorus of "Good morning, Miss Lacey."

After a few minutes the headmistress came out, and said, "I have told Miss Joyce that you and I are going to have a little chat in my office. Come along."

They walked together to the tiny room that was a cupboard compared to the spacious office Miss Lacey used to have in London.

"Sit down, Mary Anne."

Marianne sat on the edge of the chair. She didn't know how she'd explain, even to Miss Lacey, who was always so fair, that she'd answered back because Miss Joyce reminded her of her math teacher in Berlin.

Miss Lacey said, "How are you getting on in your billet, Mary Anne?"

The question was so unexpected that Marianne burst into tears. "She's changed my name. She wants me to call her Mother. I can't. I have a mother, even if I don't know where she is or if she's still alive. She, that is, Mrs. Roberts, said my parents didn't want me. It's not true. She's trying to turn me into her dead child. It's awful being prayed over."

Miss Lacey offered Marianne her own handkerchief and sat in silence until Marianne was calmer.

"Why didn't you tell Miss Barry, or come to me?"

"Because I didn't want to be a nuisance."

"Will you trust me for a few days, Mary Anne? I'm sure between us, Mr. Evans and I can find the right billet for you." Miss Lacey's voice changed. "Now that we've got that out of the way, are you ready to tell me why you were sent out of class? Just the facts, Mary Anne."

"I forgot to bring in my homework, and I did badly on my test. Miss Joyce said I was lazy and that my kind take advantage. I'm sorry. I did answer back."

Miss Lacey was quiet for a moment. Her eyes looked sad. "We don't live in a perfect world, I'm afraid, and wars don't transform ideas overnight. Everyone is under stress. We are away from people we love, and it's not only children who have to adapt to unusual circumstances. You may go home at recess and bring your homework to Miss Joyce." She paused. "And Mary Anne, don't give up hope, will you?"

Miss Lacey stood up and Marianne was dismissed. She'd been really fair and understanding. Marianne knew Miss Lacey was right to tell her to hope. She'd never give up hoping her mother would find her.

Marianne allowed herself to dream for a while. She knew it wasn't possible, not in wartime, but suppose, what if by some miracle, Mutti *had* escaped?

On Friday, three days after her interview with Miss Lacey, Marianne was told she was going to a new billet.

When she got back at lunchtime, her suitcase stood at the bottom of the stairs. Uncle Dai was waiting for her.

"You're being moved," he said. "For the best it is. The neighbors have been talking about us taking in a girl from Germany. Not right, is it, when we're at war? 'Harboring an enemy,' Blodwen Jenkins said." His voice grew cold. "And what have you been telling them in that posh school of yours? Tell me that, Mary Anne."

Auntie Vi came down the stairs. "I've put Elisabeth's room straight. Just the way it was." She looked at Marianne. "And there I was thinking you were like my Elisabeth. You were going to be our own little girl."

Marianne said, "I am very sorry, Auntie Vi, Uncle Dai. But I can't be your little girl because I belong to someone else."

"Not good enough to shine our Elisabeth's shoes, you are. Go on, wait outside, wicked, ungrateful evacuee. I don't want you in my house. Blodwen Jenkins warned me we'd be sorry taking in a foreigner."

Marianne stumbled out, clutching her suitcase. The front door shut.

The curtains on both sides of number sixty-six parted. The neighbors stared at her. If she'd been a bit younger, Marianne might have put out her tongue. She felt sorry for Mr. and Mrs. Roberts, but relieved to be out of that suffocating house. Marianne sat down on her suitcase to wait. *Poor Mr. Evans, he must be tired of trying to find me a permanent billet. I hope he won't be too disappointed with me.*

"Diolch yn fawr"

A small car stopped across the street. Mr. Evans got out and called to her: "I'm in a hurry, Mary Anne. Get in quick, in the front seat next to me. That's right. Been waiting long, have you? There's cold it is for November." He hummed *"Sospan Fach."*

Marianne said, "Please, Mr. Evans, I'm sorry I'm causing you so much trouble." She bit her thumbnail.

"No trouble, *bach*, it's what I'm here for. Better luck next time."

Marianne wondered how many next times there could be.

"Here you are, then. Out you get. Don't forget your case."

"But Mr. Evans, this is the railway station. Where am I going?"

She wondered if her new billet was far away. How would she get to school, then?

"No need to look so worried. Someone's looking forward to meeting you. In the ladies' waiting room, she is. Off you go and get acquainted. I'll be along in a minute. Got to see the stationmaster." Mr. Evans went off waving cheerfully.

It's all very well for him, he doesn't have to start all over again with another new family.

Marianne had never been inside the ladies' waiting room before. She opened the door cautiously, half hoping her new foster mother hadn't arrived yet. It would be nice to have a few minutes to prepare herself.

A cloud of thick greenish-gray smoke hung in the air. It almost obliterated the tiny fire that someone must have just lit in the small grate. A woman in a dark coat and hat stood warming her hands in front of the orange glow that did not yet offer warmth or heat to brighten the gloomy room.

"Excuse me, please," Marianne said. "Are you the lady who's expecting me? Mr. Evans told me to wait in here. He'll be along in a minute."

The woman turned around slowly, and took a step towards Marianne. For a moment they looked at each other without speaking.

"Mutti, is it you? Are you real?"

"Marianne, you've got so tall."

"I knew you'd come – I always knew you'd find me." Marianne wiped her eyes on her sleeve. "The smoke's making my eyes water," she said.

"Mine, too," said her mother, and then Marianne hugged her as if she'd never let her go.

When Mr. Evans came back, Marianne and her mother were sitting very close together. They didn't notice the billeting officer until he coughed to get their attention. "Train to London's due in five minutes. Off you go with your mother, *bach*. Take your case. Permanent it is this time, Mary Anne." He smiled at them both.

On the platform Marianne said, "Mr. Evans, how did you manage it?"

"I didn't know anything myself until this morning, *bach*. No one did. Your mother just turned up. A very nice surprise, indeed. Mind you, Mary Anne, Mrs. Evans will be disappointed. Determined she was that I should buy a bed for the parlor so you could stay with her. There's happy she'll be for you both." He smiled.

Mrs. Kohn said, "You are a kind good man. Thank you."

They shook hands.

Mr. Evans helped them onto the train.

"*Diolch yn fawr* – Thank you very much, Mr. Evans," said Marianne.

The train was packed with men and women in uniform. A soldier got up and offered Mrs. Kohn his seat, and went to stand in the corridor beside Marianne. Every few minutes she checked to make sure her mother was still there, that she hadn't imagined the last hour. When the train stopped at Cardiff, several people got out, and at last Marianne could sit with her mother.

"I brought some sandwiches. You must be hungry." Mrs. Kohn unwrapped a small neat package.

"*Mother*, how do you expect me to eat? I'm bursting with questions. I want you to tell me every tiny detail right from the beginning – how you got to England, how you found me, and what took you so long," Marianne said.

169

"First, eat. We have plenty of time," Mrs. Kohn said affectionately.

That was the moment Marianne knew she hadn't been dreaming. Her mother was really here!

There were government signs in the compartment: CARELESS TALK COSTS LIVES, and HITLER WILL SEND NO WARNING — SO ALWAYS CARRY YOUR GAS MASK.

A sailor in the corner was fast asleep. Three young nurses were laughing and talking to each other. Mrs. Kohn looked around nervously.

"It's alright, Mutti," said Marianne. "Please don't keep me in suspense any longer. It was a delicious sandwich. I'll even eat another one."

"Oma and Opa are well, and send their love. The house was requisitioned. We expected that. They were moved to another part of the city, to a room. I got my visa stamped after I'd almost given up hope. It was on August 31st."

"That was the day I looked for you at the station. I'd dreamt about you coming to England. I was so sure you'd get there." Marianne squeezed her mother's hand.

Mrs. Kohn continued, "I finally arrived in London on Saturday, September 2nd – one day before war was declared. I was so excited knowing I'd see you."

"By then I was already in Wales," Marianne interrupted.

"If I'd only known that," her mother said. "When I got to 12 Circus Road, the house was closed up. There was no one next door to ask what had happened. I found my way to the school.

The sign on the gate read: EVACUATED TILL FURTHER NOTICE. Marianne, I can't begin to tell you how I felt." She looked away.

"Go on," said Marianne.

"I could do nothing more that day. Mrs. Davy was expecting me. I had another train to catch."

"Do you like her? What's the house like?" Marianne was eager to know all about her mother's new life.

"Mrs. Davy is a wonderful person. I enjoy working for her. The house has a beautiful garden. It was full of roses when I came. I have two small rooms for myself, a bedroom and a little sitting room. I can't wait to share them with you.

"One day Mrs. Davy came into the kitchen. I was baking an apple cake, and Mrs. Davy said to me, 'How your family must miss your cooking, my dear, and your wonderful coffee.' I couldn't speak for a moment."

"Admit it, you cried, didn't you, Mutti?" said Marianne.

"Yes. She made me tell her everything. How terrible it was not knowing how to find you. She said, 'Mary Anne must have made some friends. Surely their parents would know where the girls are?'

"I ran upstairs to get your letters. I did not have Bridget's address, but you had written her name, and that her father was a doctor. The rest was easy. Dr. O'Malley contacted Bridget in Canada, and Mrs. Davy came with me to the police station to explain to the sergeant why I needed another travel permit."

"I don't understand, Mutti."

"Aliens over sixteen are not allowed to move more than five miles away from their homes without permission. It's a sensible precaution in wartime. Before I left, Mrs. Davy said, 'Be sure to bring Mary Anne back with you. It will be so nice to have a child in the house again.'"

"I'm not a child," said Marianne. "I'll be thirteen next year."

"You haven't changed a bit. You still have an answer for everything," said her mother lovingly.

Why haven't we spoken about Vati? Marianne looked at her mother. There were lines on her face that hadn't been there a year ago.

Marianne took out the card that her father had sent her just before the outbreak of war. She gave it to her mother to read. Mrs. Kohn looked at the brief message and then sat quietly for a moment, just holding the card.

"It's only good-bye until after the war," Marianne said. "It's not forever. We'll see him again, won't we, and Oma and Opa and Ruth?"

The train lurched to a stop.

The all clear sounded, welcoming them to London.

AFTERWORD

Remember Me is a work of fiction, set against the backdrop of events that surrounded the beginning of the Second World War (1939–1945).

History is unalterable, and the facts are true, though Marianne's story is imaginary – one that children like her might have experienced.

The last *Kindertransport* left Berlin on August 31, 1939. The rescue operation had continued since December 2, 1938 and saved 10,000 children from Germany, Austria, Poland, and Czechoslovakia before international borders were closed.

Typical foster parents, who opened their homes to the young refugees, were average English people who did not speak German, and whose knowledge of the terrible events that were taking place in Europe was gleaned from occasional newspaper reports. Many of the homes were non-Jewish.

In 1945, the end of the war revealed that countless Jewish families had not survived, and many of the *Kinder* did not see their parents and relatives again.

Irene Kirstein Watts arrived in England from Berlin on December 10, 1938 by *Kindertransport*. On September 1, 1939 the eight year old became one of thousands of evacuees sent away from London and the threat of aerial bombardment to the protection of strangers in the country.

Also by Irene N. Watts

Good-bye Marianne

As autumn turns into winter in 1938 Berlin, Marianne Kohn's life begins to crumble. First there was the burning of the neighborhood shops. Then her father, a mild-mannered bookseller, must leave the family and go into hiding. No longer allowed to go to school or even sit in a café, Marianne's only comfort is her beloved mother. Things are bad, but could they get even worse? Based on true events, this fictional account of hatred and racism speaks volumes about both history and human nature.

Winner of

THE GEOFFREY BILSON AWARD FOR HISTORICAL FICTION
FOR YOUNG PEOPLE
and
THE ISAAC FRISCHWASSER MEMORIAL AWARD FOR
YOUNG ADULT FICTION.